'Dammit, Dani—' Josh began, but this time she wasn't going to take no for an answer—not when it was obviously what they both wanted.

Her mind wasn't really on what she was saying. What did conversation matter when she was finally where she'd wanted to be for so many years?

And it felt so good.

Ever since she'd first fallen in love with him she'd imagined what it would feel like when he finally held her in his arms, but this surpassed anything she'd ever dreamed. He was so tall and strong—the sort of solid bulwark that a woman could depend on to protect her when life turned rough.

'Dani...' he muttered, almost incoherently, and his head swooped down towards her even as he swept her up into his arms and pressed his lips to hers.

At last!

Josie Metcalfe lives in Cornwall with her long-suffering husband. They have four children. When she was an army brat, frequently on the move, books became the only friends that came with her wherever she went. Now that she writes them herself she is making new friends, and hates saying goodbye at the end of a book—but there are always more characters in her head, clamouring for attention until she can't wait to tell their stories.

Recent titles by the same author:

SHEIKH SURGEON CLAIMS HIS BRIDE*
THE DOCTOR'S BRIDE BY SUNRISE*
TWINS FOR A CHRISTMAS BRIDE
A MARRIAGE MEANT TO BE

Brides of Penhally Bay

*Look out for the second book
in Josie Metcalfe's neonatal duet—
coming soon from Medical™ Romance*

A WIFE FOR THE BABY DOCTOR

BY
JOSIE METCALFE

First published in Great Britain 2008
Large Print edition 2009
Harlequin Mills & Boon Limited,
Eton House, 18-24 Paradise Road,
Richmond, Surrey TW9 1SR

© Josie Metcalfe 2008

ISBN: 978 0 263 20527 5

Set in Times Roman 16½ on 19¼ pt.
17-0809-49462

Harlequin Mills & Boon policy is to use papers that are
natural, renewable and recyclable products and made
from wood grown in sustainable forests. The logging and
manufacturing process conform to the legal environmental
regulations of the country of origin.

Printed and bound in Great Britain
by CPI Antony Rowe, Chippenham, Wiltshire

A WIFE FOR THE
BABY DOCTOR

CHAPTER ONE

JOSH peered cautiously through the window in the door that barred the entrance to the unit, wary in case it was that fierce senior sister on duty.

He knew that his mother preferred to collect him from the homework club at school rather than have him walk for five minutes to the hospital on his own; knew he wasn't really supposed to come up here to wait for her shift to end; and he definitely shouldn't know the code to let himself into the unit, but he was so fascinated by the tiny babies she cared for that he just couldn't resist.

'Hi, Josh,' called one of his mother's friendlier colleagues, looking across at him from her position at the desk. He breathed a sigh of relief when he saw her welcoming smile. With Sally

Nugent on duty he knew he wasn't going to be summarily ejected tonight. 'Your mum's nearly finished. Go on into the staff lounge while you're waiting for her. There might even be some biscuits left in the tin.'

His stomach was empty but it was easy to ignore it when there was the fascinating world of medicine surrounding him. He might only be nine, but he already knew what he wanted to do when he grew up.

'Have you had any new babies in today?' he asked, lingering beside the desk while Sally frowned at something on the computer screen.

'Not so far,' she said with a distracted smile in his direction, just as the phone began to ring.

Josh could only hear Sally's side of the conversation but he could tell from the expression on her face that she was being told something serious. Usually Sally could manage to find a reassuring smile for everyone, no matter what was happening in the unit. This time he could tell from the way she suddenly went white that something very different had happened.

She clattered the phone down almost before she'd finished speaking, and instead of hurrying him through to wait out of sight in the staff waiting room—the way she normally would—she sat there for several seconds, biting her lip, apparently unable to bring herself to look in his direction.

Suddenly he felt sick with apprehension.

'Sally?' he prompted, hating the fact that his voice still sounded like a kid's when he'd been the man of the house from the moment he'd been born. Had something happened to his mother? She and Pammy were all he had in the world, at least until Pammy's baby arrived. 'What's the matter? What's going—?'

'I'm sorry, Josh,' she interrupted abruptly, getting to her feet. 'You're going to have to leave the unit. Go down and wait in the main recep-tion area.' She started ushering him towards the door. 'Your... There's an emergency coming in and your...your mother's going to need to stay on late tonight. Is there someone who can come and fetch you...to take you home?'

He knew she wasn't telling him the truth—at

least, not the whole truth—and he dug his feet in, refusing to move another inch until he had an answer to the most important question.

'Is it Mum? Has something happened to her?' he demanded, a strange shaky feeling starting deep inside him. It was the same feeling that he'd got the day his mother had phoned to tell him there had been an accident and she was delayed in A and E.

He'd been so convinced she'd been injured that initially he hadn't been able to hear her telling him that she'd been nothing more than a by-stander and was taking care of the victim's children until their father arrived. He'd known then just how devastating it would be if anything were to happen to his mother or to her best friend, Pammy. The three of them had been together all his life and were the only family he had in the world.

'Please, Sally. You have to tell me,' he demanded hoarsely, his heart beating so fast that it felt as if it was going to choke him. 'Has something happened to Mum? Is she ill? Hurt?'

'No, Josh. It's nothing like that,' she said firmly, giving his arm a squeeze, and the fact that she met his eyes this time reassured him that she was telling him the truth. 'Your mother's fine, but she's…she's going to be very busy for a while. It would be better if you went out of the unit to wait, just until—'

The sound of the lift arriving only a few feet away had her breaking off with a soft curse under her breath, and he knew that whatever had her so jumpy was about to emerge from those doors.

There was a confused cacophony of voices and noises, with orders being snapped and vital signs being monitored by bleeping machinery. As the trolley began to emerge through the gaping doorway he could see that the figure on it was having some sort of a fit, like that boy in the top class at school who'd had an epileptic attack in the gym last term. Then he heard someone using the keys he'd pressed to unlock the door into the unit, and out of the corner of his eye saw the unit's senior consultant stride into view.

'Is this Pamela Dixon?' he demanded, and Josh

gasped as if he'd been winded by a punch. 'Take her straight along to Theatre,' the man ordered briskly after a lightning-quick assessment right there in the corridor. 'Bloods *have* been taken for cross-matching, I hope?'

'What's wrong with Pammy?' Josh demanded loudly, completely forgetting that he wasn't even supposed to be there. 'Her baby's not coming for weeks yet. What are you doing to her?'

'Josh…! Hush!' He knew the feel of his mother's arms as they encircled him from behind, even though she smelt of that awful disinfectant in the hand-cleansing gel and not the lavender soap he'd bought her for her birthday. 'Pam collapsed while she was out shopping. Mr Kasarian is going to try to help her.'

'But, *Mum*, he said to take her to Theatre and Pammy *can't* have an operation,' he insisted, looking up into eyes the same golden brown as the ones that met him in the bathroom mirror when he brushed his teeth. Suddenly everything inside him clenched tight as he realised this was the first time he'd ever seen those eyes filled with fear—the same fear that was gripping him by the throat and turning his innards to water. 'He *can't* do it! It might hurt the baby.'

He tried to step forward to stop them pushing the trolley to the other end of the department, towards the one part of the unit that he'd never been allowed to investigate, but his mother held him back.

'Josh, you don't understand,' she said with a quiver in her voice. 'Mr Kasarian *has* to operate. He's trying to save Pam's life.'

'But…I don't understand.' He was having to blink hard against the hot threat of tears. 'She was all right this morning. We had breakfast together and she said she was going to walk to the shops after I went to school. She was going to buy some things for the baby, and…and…'

The expression on his mother's face evaporated the words off his tongue, the desperation there telling him that, no matter what he said, it wasn't going to change what was happening now.

'She collapsed in the shop, Josh…in the ladies' toilets… And nobody knew she was there until the cleaner heard noises in the cubicle and realised that the door had been locked for a long time.'

'Wh-what's wrong with her?' His heart felt as if it was fluttering wildly against his ribs, like the little bird that he'd rescued from next-door's cat. It was going so fast that it was making him feel quite light-headed, as if he was going to be sick. 'What's he going to do to her?'

'Her blood pressure's gone up much too high—it's called eclampsia and that's why she collapsed,' she explained briefly, and he was struck that, even now, she'd remembered that he always wanted to know *why* things happened. 'And the only way to make the blood pressure come down is to take the baby out of her... quickly.'

'But, Mum, you said...' His thoughts were such a panicky jumble that it was hard to find the words he needed first. 'The baby...Pammy's baby! It isn't time for it to come out yet.' Her face looked all blurry as he tried to put his thoughts in order, so he knew he was crying now, but he couldn't help it. Ever since he'd been told that his mother's best friend in all the world was expecting a baby he'd been so…so excited. And as soon as Pammy had told him that he was going to be able to help her to look after it…to feed it and protect it…it was all he'd been able to think about.

None of them knew whether it was a girl or a boy… Pammy said she wanted to wait until the baby was born to find out, the way she always waited till Christmas morning to open her presents. Josh had already persuaded her that it should be called Daniel if it was a boy, but if it was born too soon, it wouldn't be able to live and it wouldn't matter what it was called because it would never survive long enough to know that he would have been the best big brother ever.

'Josh, they *have* to operate,' his mother said in a funny choked voice, and he felt even worse when he saw that she was crying, too. She and Pammy had known each other for hundreds of years…ever since they'd met in that group home when they were little. They always said that they might not have been born sisters, but they were sisters now. Better than sisters.

'If they don't operate quickly, Pam will die,' she continued urgently. 'She might die even if they do, and then the baby would die, too, so Mr Kasarian really doesn't have any choice.'

He flung himself into her arms and they clung together, sobbing and terrified that they were going to lose the only family they had in the world.

'I'm sorry, Sister Weath—Meredith,' Mr Kasarian interrupted himself, the grey pallor of defeat dulling his stubble-darkened golden skin and robbing his dark eyes of their usual sparkle.

Josh had never seen him like this before; had usually seen him smiling as he answered one of the millions of questions Josh peppered him with, even though he wasn't supposed to be visiting the unit. 'Even though Pam didn't work in this particular department, she was one of ours, too, so you know that we did everything we could...'

'Of course you did,' his mother agreed softly from behind a shaky hand, her other hand tightening painfully around Josh's. He didn't care how tight she squeezed. Nothing could hurt worse than the pain inside him.

'If only someone had found her sooner,' the consultant continued. 'By the time we got her to Theatre she'd already been convulsing for so long that...' He shook his head. 'She was already going into multi-organ failure. All we could do was to try to save the baby.'

'So they're both dead,' his mother mourned, her voice so choked with tears that Josh could hardly understand the words. 'My best friend and her baby, both gone in one day when we'd got so many plans to—'

'No!' the consultant interrupted, suddenly quite flustered. 'I'm *so* sorry, Meredith. I can't have made myself clear. I lost your friend, but her baby is still alive...for the moment, at least.'

'What? It's alive?' Josh wasn't certain whether *he'd* spoken or if it had been his mother.

'Yes, Josh. It was a little girl, and she's very small, but she's a real fighter.'

'A girl!' Josh didn't know whether to be disappointed that it hadn't been Daniel, the little brother he'd wanted, or just to be pleased that Pammy's baby was still alive.

'Can we see her?' his mother asked, and for one horrified moment Josh thought she was asking to see Pammy, and the idea that he might see the woman who had been an extra mother to him the whole of his life lying there, dead, made him feel sick.

'Of course you can, Meredith,' the consultant said with a reassuring smile, and with a silent sigh of relief, Josh realised that he and his mother were talking about the baby. 'Just as soon as she's been settled in the unit and... well, I don't need to tell you any of that,' he added with a shrug. 'You probably know just as much about that side of things as I do...probably more. You've been working in the unit long enough.'

'Oh, Josh,' his mother murmured when Mr Kasarian left, and when he saw her eyes filling with tears again a feeling of panic filled him in an overwhelming flood.

All his life it had been the three of them coping together against the world, him, his mum and

Pammy. He'd never known his own father because he'd died in a motorcycle accident before he'd been born, and he'd never met the father of Pammy's baby either, but there'd never been a time when Pammy hadn't been there to help him cheer his mother up when she was sad. Now there was only him, and he had no idea what to say to stop her crying, not when he felt so much like giving in to the tears, too.

'We'll manage, Mum,' he said shakily as he patted her arm, wishing he believed it even as he voiced the words that Pammy had always said. 'We're the three musketeers, remember? And we'll *still* be the three musketeers...only this time I won't be the youngest.'

'The three musketeers,' Josh murmured as he hung his stethoscope around his neck and stuffed a notepad in the pocket of his white coat. 'What on earth made me think of that today?'

That scene had taken place at least twenty-seven years ago and had been a pivotal point in his life. The first moment he'd seen that tiny, almost transparent scrap of a baby he'd known exactly what branch of medicine he wanted to concentrate on when he was all grown up.

It must have taken some determination on his mother's part to survive in those early years, going from a household consisting of one child supported by two wage earners to one of two children supported by just one SCBU nurse. He never did know how she'd persuaded the authorities to allow her to adopt Pammy's baby, but he did know that she was a formidable woman when she set her mind to something. By his early teens he'd become very adept at finding employers who would overlook the fact that he was underage for a job by playing on the fact that he was tall and blessed with a responsible attitude. But even though he was helping to support their little family, nothing was allowed to interfere with his grades at school; nothing was permitted to get in the way of his eventual acceptance into medical school and the first step on the road to becoming a paediatric consultant.

The ring of the phone dragged him out of his unaccustomed ramble down memory lane.

'Yes, Caitlin?'

'Dr Dixon has arrived,' his secretary told him quietly, and a quick glance at his watch reminded him that he should have been ready ten minutes ago to greet the new member of staff beginning her first day on the unit.

Exactly how many minutes had he been standing there wool-gathering when there was a whole department out there depending on his input?

'Twenty-seven years on and I still can't forget the chaos that tiny baby caused in our lives,' he complained to the walls of his cramped office, then growled at the fact that Dr Danielle Dixon would definitely get the wrong impression if she heard him talking to himself.

He strode out into the corridor, trying to ignore the fact that he hadn't a clue whether it was dread or excitement that was filling his stomach with butterflies.

'I'm a consultant, for heaven's sake,' he muttered crossly as he strode out of the room. A relatively new one, admittedly, but as far as could tell, he was well respected by his immediate colleagues and his peers. He certainly didn't need to worry that the newest member of the team was going to be able to find fault with anything that happened in his unit, but…

His thoughts stalled abruptly when he caught sight of the slender, almost child-like figure waiting uncertainly by the main reception desk at the entrance to the unit.

He couldn't seem to breathe for a moment as he was struck by her ethereal beauty, then couldn't help taking advantage of the fact she hadn't seen him to look his fill.

She looked as if a puff of wind would blow her away, and that impression was only compounded by the soft cloud of silvery blonde curls and deep blue eyes that made her seem as if she only needed a pair of gossamer wings to complete the picture.

Utter nonsense, he scoffed silently. You only had to take a look at that determined little chin to realise that she had enough stubbornness for a whole herd of mules. That, after all, was what it would have needed to get her to this point in her life.

'Ah, there you are, Mr Weatherby,' the receptionist said, and the newest member of his team
turned sharply towards him and almost felled
him in his tracks with a single smile.

'Josh!' she exclaimed, hurrying towards him
and clearly bubbling over with excitement.

'Dr Dixon,' he replied firmly, in spite of the
fact that his voice felt almost rusty in his throat.

He saw the split second that she realised her
faux pas and watched her deliberately replace her
happy expression with a more serious one. 'I'm
sorry. I mean, good morning, Mr Weatherby.'

The attempt at keeping her expression straight
failed in a second and he was almost tempted to
laugh out loud. That face would never be able to
hide what she was thinking and feeling, any more
than those blue eyes could stop gleaming with the
sheer joy of being alive. That was just one reason
why he would always blame himself for…

'I can't believe it, can you?' she demanded,
stepping close enough to grab his arm with
one slender hand and almost bouncing with
excitement.

Even through the thick cotton of his white coat and the thinner sleeve of his shirt he could feel the warmth of her hand, but the sensation was far closer to the sharp hum of electricity as every hair stood to attention all over his body at the innocent contact.

'I finally made it, Josh! I'm on the way to being a paediatrician. Isn't it just the most—?'

'Congratulations,' he interrupted formally, conscious of watchful eyes and wary of gossip.

As he forced himself to step back, he told himself that it was not only on his own account but for the sake of the newest member of his team. She would hardly want to be the subject of hospital gossip on her first morning.

The increased distance between them meant that she had to release her hold on him but he still had to stifle a groan at his body's instant response to the innocuous contact from her slender hand.

It was just so wrong.

This was Dani, the tiny baby he'd fallen in love with from the first moment he'd seen her in the incubator that day, and who'd been his baby sister in everything but blood and name.

And from this morning on, he reminded himself silently, she was just the latest doctor to spend six months in his department while she decided whether it was the area of medicine in which she wanted to specialise.

'Now,' he said briskly, 'if you'd like to follow me, let's see just how much you've learned.'

He turned and strode back towards the other end of the unit, cursing himself for his abruptness. Once again he'd wiped the happiness off her face as swiftly as if he'd slapped her, and that hadn't been his intention. He just couldn't cope with any physical contact between the two of them, no matter how innocuous; had deliberately avoided being anywhere in her vicinity ever since the disastrous events of her eighteenth birthday.

'I don't know how detailed a tour you were given around the unit when you came for your interview, but—'

'Josh,' she interrupted softly, her dark blue eyes

looking almost bruised. 'Is this going to be too difficult for you… having me working in your unit?'

He nearly snorted aloud at the innocence of her question.

Difficult? Try bloody impossible, especially when she stood there looking as if she was made of spun sugar and all he wanted to do was…

'You got the job on merit,' he pointed out gruffly. 'Remember? I excused myself from your interview in case my presence biased the choice of candidate. Now all you have to do is prove that the committee made the right decision.'

'But…' She paused uncertainly.

He knew he hadn't answered her question, but hoped that at least he'd been able to redirect her thoughts. Then he saw those slender shoulders straighten and that neat little chin inch up a little further, and knew she'd accepted the challenge.

He stifled a sigh, knowing that his life would have been very much easier if Dani had chosen a similar post in another hospital, but, without being big-headed about it, he knew that his unit was one of the best for the next stage of her training if she was still determined to specialise in paediatrics. That was especially true if she was leaning towards neonatal medicine.

'This is the neonatal end of the unit,' he said crisply, unable to prevent the touch of pride in his tone, 'and it's the most recent development within the department.'

'Did it take you long to get approval?' Those dark blue eyes were visually cataloguing the set-up, from the individual prettily-curtained bays—all occupied at the moment—to the mind-boggling array of monitoring equipment surrounding each clear acrylic isolette.

'Long enough, but it was securing the level of financing that was the biggest headache. There's just so much specialist equipment needed and the cost of each item is astronomical.'

'That always seems so strange to me,' she said thoughtfully. 'When the cost of electronic items on the high street has come down so much, why should similar items be so inordinately expensive when they're being sold to hospitals?'

He was unsurprised that she should have the same niggling suspicions that he'd been harbouring for years. It just didn't seem credible that so many extra millions could be poured into a system and do so little good.

But that wasn't the issue, here, he reminded himself sternly. He'd always known that she was ready to take issue with any injustice she uncovered, right from kindergarten age, and he was struck with a sudden desire to test the mettle of this new member of his team to see whether she had changed. This was no longer a matter of girls being prevented from joining the boys' football team but the hidebound monolith of the NHS she was criticising. How would she defend her contentious words?

'You make it sound as if hospital suppliers are profiteering at the government's expense—or that those in charge of the hospital's finances aren't doing their job properly,' he commented quietly. 'Either of those scenarios would be one heck of an accusation.'

'If I *were* making an accusation,' she countered calmly. 'All I'm saying is that it seems very strange that in the same week that I bought my brand-new top-of-the-line flat-screen computer monitor, the ward I was working on at my last hospital received a similar but several-years-out-of-date model costing three times the price.'

So, his new colleague wasn't easily flustered, he noted with pleasure, and she still had the keen eye for finances that was the result of the less-than-opulent upbringing that her good-quality clothing would suggest. Interesting.

The sudden intrusion of one of the babies' monitors drew their attention and he led the way across to one of the unit's most recent patients.

They were just in time to see the nurse flick the bottom of the baby's tiny foot, then reach up to reset the monitor.

'She just needed to be reminded to keep breathing,' she said with a smile, before her gaze strayed to the woman standing at his side.

'Nadia, this is Dr Danielle Dixon. She has just joined us this morning.' He turned towards Dani, careful not to meet those stunning blue eyes. 'Nadia is one of our most experienced NICU nurses.'

'Pleased to meet you, Nadia. Call me Dani,' she said with that smile that came all the way from her heart. For a second her hand came up as if she was going to offer it in a shake, then she shook her head with a self-deprecating laugh. 'One of these days I'll remember that people wearing gloves don't want to contaminate themselves by shaking hands.'

'Believe me, it won't take long,' Nadia promised wryly. 'That antiseptic-antibiotic gel we have to use on our hands is so vicious that we learn to avoid any unnecessary contact very quickly. Another nurse in the unit had to give up nursing because her hands were permanently raw and bleeding and she just couldn't stand it any more.'

'They're trialling some new products at the moment,' Josh offered. 'Apparently, the hospital has received so many complaints that they've been forced into it, but they've got to make sure that the new products are at least as good at preventing cross-infection as the gel before they can sanction their use.'

'In the meantime, in the interest of patient safety, the staff has to put up with the status quo, even though the discomfort is more likely to make them want to skip using the stuff causing the problem,' Nadia pointed out.

'Well, I hope you're not implying that any of *my* staff are getting into slipshod habits,' Josh demanded grimly. 'If I thought that these tiny people were being put at risk by—'

'Not a chance,' Nadia interrupted with a quick smile. 'You've hand-picked every one of them, so you know they're not going to let you down.' She turned her attention to Dani. 'I hope you realise the impossible standards you're going to have to achieve to keep up with this man.'

Josh couldn't miss the gleam in those dark blue eyes as she met his gaze head on.

'I've heard all about Mr Weatherby,' she said quietly. 'And even though I might not come up to his exacting expectations *yet*, it doesn't mean that I'd ever give up trying.'

There was something in her expression that he couldn't read and there was definitely something in the determination in her voice that told him she was delivering a personal message, but with Nadia as an onlooker this wasn't the right time to ask what that message was. The last thing either of them needed was gossip and speculation about the two of them.

She didn't know what impulse had her sending the message, but even though she was exhausted by a very long first day in her new job, she hadn't been able to resist when she'd checked her computer for messages and seen that he was logged on.

DaniD: Are you still speaking to me, BB?

Then, of course, she'd had to sit there, almost holding her breath while she waited to see if he would answer.

Had she made a monumental mistake in applying for the post?

It was all she'd ever wanted to do, but after that

disastrous episode on her eighteenth birthday...
all her own fault, of course...things had never
been the same between the two of them since. If
she'd made everything worse by—

BB: What's the matter, DaniD? Have you
forgotten that I'm more likely to shout at you
than go silent?

She was so relieved that he'd answered that her
eyes were actually burning with the threat of tears.

DaniD: Not the strong silent type, then?
BB: Hardly!

She could almost hear his huff of laughter. He'd
always been so driven to succeed in whatever he
set his heart on that he definitely wasn't the sort
to suffer fools gladly. She could imagine that his
reputation as a perfectionist was well earned.

BB: Having second thoughts?
DaniD: About what?

BB: The job.
DaniD: No! None!

Well, that wasn't quite true.

She certainly didn't have any regrets about her choice of career. It was early days yet, but so far it looked as if it was going to be everything she'd always imagined it would be.

No, the doubts were of a more personal kind, and something that really couldn't be shared with the man who'd dubbed himself BB…her big brother…from the moment she'd been born.

Except she hadn't seen him as a brother at all since long before her eighteenth birthday, while he never saw her as anything other than the little helpless girl he had to look after…even though she was now twenty-seven.

BB: Get some sleep. Tomorrow won't be any easier.

She growled aloud when she read the message. It could have been sent to an immature teenager needing a prod to send her to bed for the night, and sent her angrily scrolling across for the icon to close the messenger function on the screen. When would he ever admit that she was now an adult and could decide for herself when it was time to go to sleep? She—

Just before she could click the annoying man into oblivion he sent again.

BB: You did well today, Dani, especially getting that IV in first time. See you tomorrow.

She sat back and stared at the final message he'd sent before severing the connection and couldn't help the satisfied grin that crept over her face.

She'd been proud of herself for getting that right, especially with him hovering over her shoulder. That fragile vein couldn't have been much thicker than a thread of cotton and she'd been certain that everyone could see that her hands were shaking with nerves, but the needle had gone in as easily as if she'd been doing it for years.

'So, my first day wasn't too bad,' she murmured

aloud as warmth spread through her at his praise. 'Well, that's stage one of the master plan under way. By the time the next six months are over, I'll know whether I'm on track towards a paediatric consultancy.'

She pulled a face when a familiar voice in the corner of her mind said, *She's always been determined to follow in her big brother's footsteps, ever since she learned to walk.*

'Oh, Mum, if only you knew,' she said on a sigh, smiling when she remembered the last time she'd seen Meredith Kasarian, the only mother she'd ever known.

Josh's mother had only been persuaded to take early retirement when the consultant who had tried to save Pam Dixon's life all those years ago had finally convinced her to marry him.

Meredith had always been the sort to put on a cheerful face…but it had been a real eye-opener to see the soft expression in her eyes as she'd gazed at her new husband and to see her blushing like a girl when he'd claimed her with a kiss at the end of the wedding ceremony.

'That's what I want, too,' Dani whispered wistfully, far from certain that she would ever achieve it. After all, there was a huge obstacle in her way by the name of Joshua Weatherby.

She cringed when she remembered her first attempt at telling him about her dream, and mourned the death of the closeness they'd shared for the first eighteen years of her life. From that day on, he had erected an impenetrable barrier between the two of them, preventing her from sharing anything but the most superficial of social conversations.

'Well, I've got six months to change his mind,' she declared aloud, needing to hear the words bounce back at her from the bland walls of her tiny staff flat to bolster her determination.

Even so, she couldn't help wondering just how different the last few years would have been if she hadn't drunk that glass of birthday champagne to bolster her courage before she'd spoken to him.

CHAPTER TWO

'AND what are you doing in here, young man?' said a voice over Josh's shoulder. After an initial start of surprise, he relaxed and smiled, knowing that the apparently gruff words would be accompanied by a twinkle in the consultant's dark eyes.

'I'm visiting my sister while I wait for Mum to finish work,' he explained, then held up his hands. 'I scrubbed and used the hand gel and haven't touched anything I shouldn't.'

'Good. Good,' Mr Kasarian said seriously. 'And how is our patient doing today?'

'Much better,' Josh said with a beaming smile. 'When she was first born I didn't know if she would stay alive… well, she was just so tiny, like a little bird that fell out of its nest before it grew any feathers.'

The consultant chuckled. 'That's exactly what they look like when they're that small,' he agreed.

'And then she kept forgetting to breathe, and Sally showed me how to flick her under her foot to remind her, but she hasn't needed to be reminded for a whole day... And she's put on some weight, too!' Josh couldn't believe how much better he'd felt when he'd seen that little rise on the weight graph. It was as if that tiny gain had given him permission to believe that they weren't going to lose Pammy's baby, too.

'There's something else that we've noticed,' Mr Kasarian said, drawing him out of his thoughts. 'Look up at the monitor screen next time you come to visit your sister and see what happens when you start to talk to her. Sally was watching the other day and saw a change in her pulse and respirations...her breathing.'

'And that's a bad thing?' Josh felt as if he'd been kicked in the stomach. The last thing he wanted was for his visits to make the baby sick. He knew from what his mum told him that the unit was always busy and there was never enough time to spend with her little patients. All he'd wanted to do was let the baby know that he was her big brother and he was there for her, but if coming to see her was causing her harm…

'Not at all!' Mr Kasarian exclaimed heartily. 'It's good. Very good. It seems as if she already recognises your voice, and her heart and her breathing are stronger when you're with her.'

It almost felt as if his own heart was swelling in his chest and for a horrible moment he thought he was going to cry.

'Really?' he croaked with a mixture of pleasure and disbelief, for once not caring that his voice still sounded like a childish squeak. 'She knows when I'm here?'

'Check it for yourself when you come next time,' Mr Kasarian said with a smile. 'Watch the readouts on the monitors when you start speaking to her and you'll see what we mean.'

'Don't be afraid to talk to him,' Dani encouraged the terrified new mother as she hovered at the side of the high-tech isolette.

'But he's so small,' Linda Prentiss whispered as tears welled up in her bloodshot eyes, evidence of the hours of crying she'd done since her tiny son, James, had been born. 'And he jumps at noises.'

'Sudden loud noises will do that to them, the same way it does with us. Just keep your voice to a gentle murmur. That way you won't overload his little system.'

'Surely it's too early for him to be able to take anything in,' she argued softly. 'I wouldn't want to do anything that might hurt him.'

'Actually, it will probably do him a power of good,' Josh interrupted, although Dani had known he was nearby. Her whole body seemed to be tuned in to his presence whenever he was near. 'He already knows your voice, from all those months inside you. You'll be reassuring him that you're still close by in this big scary world.'

'How can you possibly know that he recognises my voice?' she challenged, the expression on her face a confusing mixture of hope and disbelief. 'My in-laws are saying that he's already so badly brain damaged that he'll never be any better than a vegetable.'

'I don't believe that for a minute,' Josh reassured her. 'Of course, some very early babies do end up with permanent disabilities, especially if they have serious bleeding in their brains. But, so far, your son hasn't had any problems like that, and we're going to do our very best to help him to get out of here in the best possible health. Many premature babies go on to lead perfectly normal lives; some even become doctors and come back to take care of other premature babies, isn't that right, Dr Dixon?'

'I've heard of at least one case where that's happened,' Dani agreed, silently cursing him for putting her on the spot. He knew how easily she blushed, and the last thing she wanted was for the whole hospital to know that she'd once been a scrawny little scrap like their tiny patients. She'd far rather that they judged her on her performance as a doctor now.

'But you really think he recognises my voice?' Linda was too firmly focused on her son to have taken in any hints of a personal history. 'How can you tell?'

'The electronic equipment will tell you,' he explained, and Dani held her breath as he paused for a moment, wondering if he was going to tell their patient's mother the tale that she'd heard about all her life.

For the first time since she'd joined his team he actually allowed their eyes to meet and the feeling of connection was like an electric charge through her body.

'Next time you come into the unit, you can test it,' he continued with a slightly husky edge to his voice that told Dani he was reliving that long-ago shock of realisation. She'd first heard about it so long ago that it had always been a part of her life. 'Before you say anything to him, watch the monitors, then see what happens to his breathing and his heart rate when you start talking to him. It might take a couple more days before you can see it clearly, because he's had a traumatic few hours and needs to catch up with himself, but I shall expect a full report before the end of the week. OK?'

'OK,' she whispered, and Dani wasn't surprised to see that for the first time since her son had arrived on the unit, Linda's expression held more hope than despair.

'He's so nice,' she whispered to Dani as Josh let himself out of the room. 'From what you see on the television and in films, I thought consultants were all pompous tyrants, but he sounds as if he really understands what I'm going through; as if he really cares.'

'He's special,' Dani agreed readily, then could have kicked herself when she saw the flash of speculation in the young woman's eyes. 'As you said,' she continued hastily, 'some consultants are terrible to work with. I haven't been here long, but so far he's been fine—a good boss and a good teacher. Now, how about making yourself comfortable in that chair beside the isolette? Do you want a couple of pillows behind your back? You must still be very sore after the delivery, and your midwife will be very cross with me if I don't look after you properly.'

* * *

She hardly saw anything of Josh for the rest of that day, or the next, but that didn't mean that he wasn't constantly in her thoughts.

All it had taken was the retelling of the story of her infant self reacting to his presence to reawaken her teenage conviction that there had always been a special connection between the two of them.

As a little girl, she'd only known that Josh was the best big brother that any girl could have. He'd been endlessly patient with the way she'd slavishly followed him around, when her friends' brothers were forever telling *their* siblings that they were pests. And as for those times when she'd succumbed to a childish illness, because his…their… mother had needed to be at work, it had always been Josh's gentle ministrations that had soothed her feverish bad temper and distracted her with yet another story.

It had only been when she'd started looking at him with the new awareness of a teenager's eyes that everything had changed.

At first, she'd been frightened by the way her feelings towards her adored big brother had altered. There had been security in being his little Dani…the name he and his mother had compromised on in memory of the baby brother he'd wanted to call Daniel. The trouble was, each time he'd come home from medical school she'd seen how much he had changed while he'd been away, and even though a part of her had longed for the security of their old relationship, it had been impossible to go back.

It was only after the disaster of her eighteenth birthday that she'd realised that the changes had all been on her side. The look of horror on his face when she'd kissed him had proved that he'd been completely oblivious to the fact that she'd been growing up, that she didn't see him as just a brother any more, and that expression was something she'd never been able to forget.

So, what on earth was she doing working with the man? Was she completely mad to put herself through six months of…of what?

She forced herself to think about the situation, calmly and rationally.

For a start, there wasn't a post anywhere in the country where she would get a better grounding in her chosen field than in Josh's department. In spite of his comparative youth, there were few who could equal his knowledge or his dedication. And if that came with six months of butterflies in her stomach whenever she heard his voice, or fighting down the urge to leap on him every time she saw him and beg him to kiss her senseless? Well, that was a price she was willing to pay.

Anyway, she'd never given up hoping. If she was lucky, her protective big brother might finally come to realise that she wasn't his baby sister any more but an attractive woman who was as dedicated to her profession as he was.

'But that won't happen if I stand around with a besotted expression on my face when there are tests to perform and results to chase up,' she muttered under her breath, and had to stifle a shriek when she saw the time. She'd come in early that morning to give herself some leeway, but now there was less than an hour left before Josh started the morning's staff meeting, and the last thing she needed was to arrive late with half of the files incomplete.

Josh bent over the frail little figure in the isolette and had to work hard not to let his thoughts show on his face.

He couldn't think of anything more that any of them could have done to help this precious little boy in his fight for survival, but with every passing minute it was becoming increasingly obvious that their efforts had been in vain.

Unlike the progress James Prentiss was making, at twenty-three weeks gestation, it had already been unlikely that Max would escape unscathed if he *did* win the battle. A series of bleeds deep inside his brain had almost guaranteed that he would be severely disabled, but his parents had been so desperate that their last hope of a family should have a chance that he hadn't been able to shut their hollow-eyed expressions out of his mind long enough to sleep for more than an hour or two at a time. He hadn't even been able to force himself to go home last night and now had the stiff neck that often came as the result of dozing off in a chair.

As if standing beside him and watching as Max fought for every breath would make any difference, he berated himself silently, especially with that deadly infection rampaging through his lungs unchecked by everything they'd thrown at it.

'Max *is* going to get better, isn't he?' Letty Montgomery pleaded, but it was painfully obvious how hard she was having to work to try to sound optimistic.

'Is your husband here, Letty?' he asked, sidestepping her question with one of his own. 'He usually comes here on his way to work, doesn't he?'

'He should be here any minute,' she confirmed shakily, suddenly looking every one of her thirty-nine years as she collapsed onto the nearby chair as if her legs wouldn't hold her any more.

Josh knew that, in spite of her hopeful question, he almost didn't need to spell out the bad news. The look of misery in her eyes was mute evidence that she knew what he wanted to talk about, and that it wasn't good.

'When he arrives, would you get Dr Dixon to give me a buzz? I just need to chase up some of Max's lab results.' And take a couple of minutes to work out exactly how he was going to break the bad news.

The fact that he worked in an area of medicine where his patients often existed right on the very knife edge of survival meant that a higher proportion of them weren't going to survive. As a depressing consequence of that, he had to go through this conversation far more often than most, but it didn't matter how many times he'd had to do it, it never seemed to get any easier. In fact, he'd found out early on in his training that somehow it was always worse when it was a child involved rather than someone who had lived a long and fruitful life.

'Mr Weatherby, I think Dani went up to the lab to chase up the results,' Letty volunteered tentatively. 'She took more tests when she came in this morning.'

'Good,' Josh said with a reassuring smile even as he wondered just what time Dani had arrived that morning.

Had she even gone home last night? he pondered when he saw the dark circles under her eyes a few minutes later when she arrived in his room with a small sheaf of paperwork in her hand. It was all very well, wanting to do a good job in a new post, but she wouldn't succeed if she exhausted herself in the first few days.

'Well?' he prompted as he held out his hand for the printout of Max's results, hoping against hope that the figures would give at least some grounds for hope.

There weren't any.

'Damn,' he muttered when he saw the readings that confirmed the fact that Max's infections were growing worse instead of better. And there was absolutely nothing he could do about it. That tiny body just didn't have any spare resources to battle the invader. It had never been intended to take on such a foe at a time when it should still have been safely inside the shelter of a cosy womb.

'Josh, you *are* going to speak to them…to warn them that…?' He heard her swallow as she allowed the sentence to die away but they both knew how it would have ended. He had to warn the parents that their baby had very little time left. That it could be a matter of hours before the battle was lost.

Before he could speak there was a tentative knock at the door and Letty's pale face appeared when he called an invitation to enter.

'James has arrived,' she said. 'And Sister told me that Dr Dixon was already in here with you, so…'

'Come in, please, both of you.' He gestured towards the group of chairs in front of the window. 'Would you like a drink? Tea, coffee or…?'

'N-nothing, thank you,' Letty stammered, her eyes wide with dread. She was visibly trembling as her husband tried to guide her towards one of the chairs.

Josh couldn't help but be impressed that, even though she looked as though she would fall over at any moment, she stood her ground and forced herself to stare straight at him.

'You're going to tell us that Max is dying, aren't you?' she said in accusing tones, the very picture of a lioness defending her cub. 'You've brought us in here to tell us that you're not going to bother to do anything more to save our little boy…our precious little…'

'Shh, love. Shh,' her husband soothed as he wrapped an arm tightly around her shoulders and pressed her into the nearest chair. 'Let the man speak.'

There was something in his eyes as they met Josh's that let him know that he understood what was coming; that he'd already resigned himself to the fact that he was going to lose the only child he'd ever have.

For just a moment Josh longed to be able to give them something to hope for, but that wouldn't just be dishonest, it would also be unkind.

He flicked a glance towards Dani and wondered for an instant if she'd really thought through her career choice carefully enough. Of course there was an enormous amount of satisfaction in the work he did, but there was also so much devastation when there was absolutely nothing they could do for their tiny charges. Dani was a gentle, soft-hearted girl. Would it damage something essential inside her if she specialised in a branch of medicine where she had to deal with this sort of scene time after time?

Suddenly, he realised that the expectant silence had been going on for several beats too long while he'd been distracted with thoughts about his newest colleague. With a quick glance down at the papers in his hand to restore his focus, he deliberately stepped forward to lower himself into the chair opposite the Montgomerys and leant forward.

'Unfortunately, I haven't got anything good to report,' he admitted with an all-too-familiar ache in his heart. 'The latest test results aren't any better than before. In fact, they're worse,' he continued bluntly when Letty would have interrupted. 'Much worse because, in spite of everything we've been pumping into his system, the infection's gained so much ground that his lung function is almost zero and without oxygen getting into his system…'

'But he's got the mask on and that's connected to the oxygen...' James Montgomery might think he was holding together well, but he was just as close to the edge as his wife.

'That's true, but normally the oxygen is taken up in the lungs to be transferred into the blood and circulated around the body. In Max's case, even on the highest flow rate, the infection is preventing enough oxygen being taken up. That is pretty bad in itself, but these latest tests show us that the infection has broken through from the lungs into the blood, and has now spread throughout his body. Unfortunately, even when it was confined to his lungs we couldn't find anything to get rid of it, so we're very much afraid that it won't be long before all his organs start to shut down.'

Damn, he cursed silently. He'd had all too much practice at coping with crying patients and their families, but even over the sound of their distress he'd heard Dani gulp as she fought for some semblance of professional control, but to see the glitter of tears in her eyes was enough to choke him.

'H-how long before…before…?' James stumbled over the sound of his wife's heartrending sobs.

'It's impossible to say, but…' Josh shook his head. He'd seen some babies struggle on for days, their lives ebbing slowly away, while others went rapidly downhill, seemingly in minutes. 'Probably within hours,' he suggested gently.

'J— Mr Weatherby,' Dani corrected herself quickly. 'Would it be all right if Letty and James hold Max while he's…?'

'Of course it would,' he agreed hastily, silently kicking himself for being so distracted that he hadn't suggested it. 'We can detach a lot of tubes and wires so you can cuddle him properly.'

'And you can talk to him and tell him how much you love him,' Dani continued as she gently shepherded the two of them out of the room, the glance she threw his way over her shoulder just before she left his room so full of empathy with the couple's plight that it was almost enough to break his heart.

Four hours later, Max's fight for life was over.

In spite of his own workload, Josh had been aware that Dani had hovered just outside the isolation room for most of that time, doing whatever she could to make the grim inevitability of the baby's impending death at least a little more bearable. Tiny hand- and foot-prints had been made of the almost transparent limbs and precious photographs had been taken, for the first time without the ubiquitous evidence of all the technical efforts that had been keeping him alive.

The hospital chaplain had appeared with remarkable speed when the possibility of a christening had been mentioned, and an unbelievably tiny christening gown had appeared, apparently from thin air.

In the end, there had just been two broken-hearted people sitting side by side with an arm around each other and their son cradled between them as his tiny heart finally gave up the unequal struggle. Two people inside the room, Josh noted, but Dani was still keeping vigil outside, with her cheeks every bit as wet as theirs.

And why had he stood just out of sight in his

own doorway, stupidly wanting nothing so much as to wrap her in his arms and promise her that she'd never have to cry again?

Stupid, that was the right word to describe him. As if she'd ever accept that sort of comfort from him. After a lifetime of battling against the odds, she'd be more likely to cut him off at the knees. It was useless remembering that one lapse in judgement the night of her birthday and wishing he'd handled the situation differently. It had probably been a minor aberration fuelled by a glass or two of alcohol and she'd doubtless forgotten all about it in the years since. A girl…*woman*…who looked like Dani, and with her bubbly personality and obvious intelligence, wouldn't have been short of offers in the inter-vening years.

And the fact that he wanted to throttle any man who'd ever dared to lay a finger on her was his own stupidity.

Of course, he could always try to fool himself that it was a brother's typically over-developed need to protect his little sister, but that wouldn't account for the other feelings that swamped him every time he caught sight of her.

Enough! He cut off his spiralling thoughts fiercely, wondering how on earth he was going to survive the next six months. Now that she'd actually started on his team, it would be impossible to transfer her out of his sight without making some very embarrassing explanations, and... well, apart from seriously blighting her career, it would totally destroy his credibility as the leader of this team, to say nothing of injuring his standing within the medical community.

If it had been nothing more than the obvious age difference between the two of them, that would be bad enough as far as the gossips were concerned, but it wouldn't be something that would cause him any major problems with his colleagues. No, it was the fact that she was a junior member of his team that could potentially leave him open to accusations of sexual harassment, and while the powers that be were fully aware of the connection between the two of them, if the scandalmongers were to find out that Dani was his sister...

'You look dreadful,' he said sharply when her blotchy tear-stained face finally appeared in the doorway to his office. He was becoming more afraid by the hour that this specialty would be too much for her, and his harsh tone was the only way he could cover up the sudden ache around his heart. She'd only been on his team for a matter of days but the busy unit would seem almost empty without the possibility of finding her sunny presence around every corner.

She gasped at his words as if he'd physically struck her, then a familiar mulish expression crossed her face, followed by, 'Well, excuse me for momentarily giving way to my emotions, Mr Weatherby. Not all of us have had the operation to remove them.' And the door closed behind her with a pointed, well-controlled click that spoke more than a slam ever would.

'That went well.' He sighed harshly and rubbed both hands over his face. 'The next six months are going to be an absolute nightmare.' Especially if he was going to have to watch every word around her. 'So, what's different about that?' he grumbled. 'You've been having to watch yourself around her ever since…ever since that kiss she gave you on her eighteenth birthday.' And that was an image he didn't need to have inside his head the next time he saw her.

Thank goodness they would only be interacting in a professional capacity over the next few months. With his mother finally taking the long-delayed trip to meet her new Kasarian relatives, he wouldn't be forced to hide his feelings in a social or family context.

CHAPTER THREE

DANI watched Josh bend over the delicate little wrist, one lean-fingered hand positioning it just right while the other directed the fine surgical steel of the needle into the thread-like vein at the first attempt.

'I'm sorry, sweetheart,' he murmured when his little patient wailed fitfully. 'I didn't mean to make you cry.'

Dani couldn't help the warm feeling that spread inside her chest because she knew that he meant it. He really didn't like making his little charges cry, even when the things he was doing to them were for their benefit.

'At least she *can* cry now,' she pointed out. 'When she had that tube down her throat she couldn't even let you know she wanted to complain that you were making a pincushion of her.'

'It's a strange sort of progress when you track it by the baby's ability to cry,' he said darkly, but she could tell from the golden gleam in his eyes that he was happy with little Leonie's latest milestone.

Happy enough to accept an invitation to go for a drink this evening? she wondered, but didn't fancy her chances. She'd actually thought that working with him might go some way towards helping him to see that she was a grown woman…an attractive adult who was ready, willing and able to have a relationship with him. As if that was going to happen when he spent most of the time at the other end of the department, or at least the other side of whatever room she happened to be working in.

Well, as long as he wasn't staying out of her way because she wasn't good enough to be on his team… No. If that were the case, he certainly wouldn't be taking himself off to the other end of the unit. He would be finding the fastest way to shift her into another specialty altogether. So, it must just be that she'd seriously calculated wrongly if she'd thought he was going to change his mind about her, and the important thing to do now was damage limitation. She was going to have to find some way of sitting him down to talk, and then she was going to have to find the right words to let him know that all she wanted from him was to pass on his medical expertise…

Ha! And what a lie that would be. For the last nine years every man she'd met had been measured against Josh and been found wanting, so it was highly unlikely that making a decision to become…what?…friendly col-leagues would work?

It would only work if he could somehow metamorphose into someone who didn't set her pulse racing with nothing more than the sound of his voice.

'But I have to work with him for the next six months, so I've *got* to get it under control,' she muttered through gritted teeth, even as her hackles rose at the sight of Josh smiling at one of the nurses. And that was just plain stupid. She had no right to feel jealous when it was nothing more than one of the hundreds of smiles he showered around in the course of a day…wasn't it?

Of course it was. And to prove that it didn't mean a thing to her, she was finally going to speak to the man and get their new relationship on an even footing, once and for all.

'Josh…ah, Mr Weatherby…' she corrected herself as she approached the two of them, wishing that her own legs were as long as the leggy beauty who was laughing prettily at something Josh had said. 'Excuse me, but would it be possible to have a word with you?' she asked, feeling almost like a child speaking to two grown-ups as they towered over her. It was bad enough that the top of her head barely reached Josh's heart, but to have the other woman looking down her nose at her as well.…

'Thanks for this, Gillian.' He held up some sort of binder. 'I'll let you have it back as soon as I can.'

'Let me know when you're bringing it over and I'll cook you a meal…it's the least I can do to show you how grateful I am,' the stunning

redhead purred before she undulated her way
out of the unit on legs that seemed to reach all
the way up to her armpits.

'You wanted to speak to me?' Josh said, and
she couldn't help noticing that the easy smile that
had hinted at the dimples he'd always despised
as a teenager had completely disappeared now
that he was talking to *her*.

Dani glanced around and cringed at the
number of members of staff within earshot of
the two of them. This was hardly the venue
she'd hoped for when she'd decided this conversation was necessary, but as the likelihood of
Josh agreeing to meet her for a drink at the end
of the shift was slim to non-existent, it would
have to do.

She drew in a bracing snatch of air and began
in a rush. 'I wanted to apologise. I realise it was
completely unprofessional but I can't absolutely
guarantee that it won't happen again because
even though they warned us right through our
training that we shouldn't get too emotionally
involved with our patients, I just couldn't help

it… He was such a tiny little thing and his parents were just so…'

Josh held both hands up, palms towards her, and shook his head.

'Dani, *breathe,*' he said, and her heart lifted when she heard the hint of humour in his tone. 'Come into my office, because I haven't got a clue what you're talking about.'

He led the way, his long-legged stride forcing her to trot to keep up as he detoured through his secretary's cramped space rather than accessing the room from the door in the corridor.

'Drat! I'd forgotten that Caitlin wouldn't be here,' he muttered as he dropped the glossy folder he was carrying on her desk and reached for a block of bright yellow sticky notes. For a moment there was silence while she watched his familiar slashing handwriting filling the available space, then he peeled the note off the block and stuck it on the folder. 'Drugs reps,' he growled in the same tone of voice he would use to speak about an outbreak of MRSA, and scowled darkly before leading the way into his own room. 'It doesn't matter how many times they're told to make an appointment, they still try to waylay me to persuade me that their latest wonder drug will solve all my problems.'

'Perhaps it will,' she suggested sweetly in a replay of several such conversations over the years, then had to fight the urge to grin when he turned the scowl on her.

'It might,' he admitted, 'but I'm not willing to let my fragile patients be used as guinea pigs in an unproven drugs trial just because they send a scantily clad female to offer me an all-expenses-paid holiday.'

'Very high-minded of you,' she agreed, and saw those golden eyes narrow ominously in her direction.

'Wretched girl!' he complained as he dropped wearily into the chair he'd occupied when he'd broken the bad news to Max's parents, and waved her to take one, too. 'You always did know how to wind me up. So, tell me what all that was out in the corridor just now.'

'You mean, when Miss Scanty-pants was

trying to climb all over you?' she asked with an attempt at innocence, enjoying the rare episode of light-hearted teasing between them too much to want to spoil it, even to get the necessary apology off her chest.

He scowled at her but didn't comment, opting instead to wait for her to come to the point.

'I just wanted to apologise,' she said simply. 'I realise it wasn't very professional for me to be standing around in a corridor, dripping, and I promise that it won't happen—'

'I would be most concerned if it *didn't* happen again,' he interrupted sharply. 'If you aren't the type of person who can empathise with what these families are going through, then you're not the right person to be working in *my* unit.'

'But...' she tried to interrupt, confused by his apparent about-face.

'That doesn't mean to say that you should allow your emotions to get in the way of doing your job,' he continued, totally ignoring her attempt at interruption, 'and doing it to the very best of your ability. But shedding tears is almost an occupational hazard when you're working here.'

Now she really was confused.

'Well, if you see crying as par for the course, why did you snap at me earlier if it wasn't for crying after baby Max died?'

He sighed heavily and ran his fingers distractedly through his hair, disturbing the professional-looking neatness and revealing the fact that it was definitely more than a week beyond its usual neatly barbered length. Any longer and it would start looking like a lion's mane with those natural pale streaks in the dark blond thickness of it.

'I'm sorry about that, but…' He paused and shook his head, a frown of concern etched on his forehead. 'If I snapped at you it's because I'm not certain whether this is the right specialty for you. You're so soft-hearted that you'll probably end up breaking your heart over every one of the patients and—'

'And you're so hard-bitten that you don't? Ha!' she challenged with a disbelieving laugh. 'Josh,

I've known you too long to believe that eye-wash. Don't forget, I saw you every spring when you tried to rescue the baby birds that fell out of their nests, *and* when you saw that cat hit by the car that day when you came to meet me from school. I walked all the way to the vet's with you when you carried it there to see if they could fix its leg.' Apparently, the poor creature had been so badly injured that there had been nothing the vet could do but put it out of its misery, but she could still remember the expression on Josh's face and had known that he'd taken the animal's death as a personal failure.

'That was a long time ago,' he said dismissively, but she couldn't help seeing the hint of colour that washed up over his lean cheeks.

'But you haven't really changed in all the time I've known you,' she countered. 'You still need to take care of anything smaller and weaker than yourself…whether it needs taking care of or not.' she added with a stubborn lift of her chin. 'That's the whole point of the next six months, isn't it? So that I get a solid grounding on what you do in this sort of unit, and to see if this really is where my career lies.'

'Yes, but—'

'But nothing,' she snapped, wondering how she could still find him so attractive even when she was so annoyed with him. 'Whether you like it or not, Mr Weatherby, I'm a bona fide member of your team for the next six months, and I *will* do my job to the best of my ability. And if I have to take a couple of minutes off to blow my nose and put cold water on my eyes when we lose one of the tinies, then you can dock the time from my pay, but you aren't going to frighten me off by huffing and puffing…sir!'

He gave an exasperated sigh. 'Dani, I'm not trying to frighten you off. Heaven knows, we need all the top-notch doctors we can recruit, but this is a high-stress specialty and—'

'And you don't think I'm up to it, is that it?' She could feel her blood pressure rising by the second.

'No. It's not that. It's—'

'Dammit, Josh, are you *ever* going to see that

I'm not that little scrap hanging on to life by a thread?' She barely stopped herself from shouting it at him, only just remembering in time that there was a whole busy department outside the door. 'I'm all grown up now. I'm a qualified doctor, trying to decide what specialty to follow for the rest of my career. I've got a brain and I know how to use it. I *don't* need you following me around to make sure I don't fall down and skin my knees.'

She spun round on one foot and strode swiftly out of the door, suddenly afraid that she would break the habit of a lifetime and resort to physical violence if she had to stay in the same room as him one second longer.

'This definitely wasn't a good idea,' she muttered under her breath as she filled a plastic cup with cold water, then downed it in one draught, hoping that it would cool her down.

But working in Josh's unit hadn't only been the ideal professional step for her. She'd also seen it as a last chance to build on their former relation-ship, hoping that Josh would realise that they could be something very different than brother and sister to each other.

So far, all the proximity seemed to be doing was driving a deeper wedge than ever between the two of them.

Several hours later Josh was still alternating between anger that Dani had sounded off at him in such an unprofessional way and a sneaking sense of guilt that every word she'd said had been nothing less than the truth.

The very last thing he needed was to have her tell him where to draw the line. He already knew he could be a rather overbearing big brother, but he came by those tendencies naturally—it felt as if he'd been watching over her for almost every moment of the first twenty-seven years of her life. The trouble was, he didn't dare relax his guard or who knew where they would end up. That slip on her eighteenth birthday had left her wary of him for the first time in her life, much to his dismay, and he didn't intend doing anything else to drive her away.

The alternative—losing her presence even on the edges of his world—wasn't something he liked to contemplate, so he had to keep any hint of his attraction to her buried out of sight.

'And there's no point in having her spend six months in the unit if she doesn't learn as much as possible,' he reminded himself when he contemplated locking himself away in his office for the duration. 'You're just going to have to treat her like any other new recruit to the team and get on with your job.' And forget the fact that the very molecules of the air seemed charged with electricity whenever she was there; and that his heart beat faster and every sinew and muscle seemed to grow tense when they were in the same room; and that when they touched—even the most innocently inadvertent of brushes—his body responded with the embarrassing eagerness of a teenager on a hormonal overload.

'You're talking to yourself again,' said a nearby male voice, and Josh's cheeks heated in a very juvenile way when he saw his fellow paediatrician standing in the doorway.

'Tim. I didn't hear you come in,' he said shortly, hoping it looked as if he'd been muttering over the piles of paperwork on his desk rather than one aggravating pocket-sized junior doctor.

'Caitlin said it was all right to come in as your new recruit had just left.' Tim Nuttall collapsed bonelessly into the nearest chair and stretched his lanky legs almost halfway across the available floor space. 'How's she working out so far?'

For several seconds Josh had no idea what to say. He certainly couldn't tell an inveterate gossip like Tim that the next six months were going to be purgatory on earth, and he definitely couldn't tell him why.

Unfortunately, Tim didn't need him to say a word. He was quite capable of reading meanings into even the briefest of pauses.

'I'm not surprised you're lost for words,' he said with a meaningful chuckle and a lecherous waggle of his eyebrows. 'I don't know how you're going to get anything done for the next six months with someone who looks like that on your staff.'

Twenty-seven years of practice had his protective feelings rearing up in Dani's defence.

'You know as well as I do that I wouldn't make
any untoward advances towards one of my staff—
not if I want to stay clear of harassment charges.'

'As if it never happens,' Tim scoffed. 'Why, I
could tell you of at least half a dozen "relationships" that have been going on in just the last—'

'I don't want to know,' Josh interrupted curtly.
'All that matters to me is that it won't be happening in *my* unit.'

'In that case, old man, if you'll take my advice
you'll go out as soon as possible and get yourself
thoroughly laid, because that's the only way I'd
be able to keep it zipped if I were going to be
working with that gorgeous little doll. Do you
know if she's single or…?'

'Oh, for heaven's sake, Tim. If you haven't got
anything better to talk about, I have. Was there
a serious point to this visit or can I get on with
what I was doing?'

'It seems to me that what you were doing was
sitting there muttering to yourself when I arrived

but, hey, perhaps Einstein used to do that, too…right before he worked out his theory of relativity.'

'Tim…' How could he get angry with someone who was unfailingly cheerful as well as being a good paediatrician?

To his great relief the telephone rang out a strident summons and Josh reached for it with a fervent hope that his colleague hadn't heard anything incriminating.

'Yes, Caitlin?' he said, recognising his receptionist's voice and silently cursing himself for being disappointed that it wasn't Dani. After all, it had only been minutes since she'd stalked out of his room after reading him the Riot Act. What would she be wanting to speak about with him?

'Dani said to tell you that she's on her way down to A and E. There's an RTA passenger coming in and she's seven months pregnant. Apparently, the paramedics radioed ahead to warn that she might need an emergency Caesarean.'

'Right, Caitlin, can I leave you to mobilise the

troops?' he said briskly while his pulse was still recovering from the simple fact of hearing the wretched woman's name. It would be far better for everyone if he just concentrated on the matter in hand...an injured woman whose baby might have to fight for its own survival long before its fragile system was ready for the task.

'I'll leave you to it,' Tim said as he levered himself out of the chair. 'I was only going to ask if I can put your name down for the hospital's fundraising squash tournament.'

Josh pulled a face but before he could refuse Tim continued. 'I know this obviously isn't the right moment for this, so take some time to think about it. You don't need to make a decision till the end of the week, and the money will be coming to our end of the hospital this time, so it's in both our best interests to show support.'

'I'm unlikely to have the time,' Josh warned over his shoulder as he pulled the door closed and set off along the corridor towards the stairs.

'It's more likely that you're afraid to show off how unfit you are now that you're getting older,'

Tim taunted, secure in the knowledge that he was all of two years younger, then added slyly, 'But I'm sure you wouldn't say no to the new equipment you could buy. As I say, let me know by the end of the week...and good luck with your patient.'

He was going to need more than luck with this one, Josh realised when he took another appalled look at the woman's injuries, blocking out her feeble moans of distress for the safety of her baby.

'How long before you're ready to put her under?' he demanded, even as he reached out to check the positioning of the foetal monitor and found Dani's hand there before him.

'Go and get scrubbing,' she muttered, almost shouldering him out of the way. 'Someone from Orthopaedics is on their way, so is a vascular surgeon. And there's one of the unit's newest humidicribs warming all ready for the baby, Nadia is ready to special the baby as soon as you get it out, and ICU and Maternity will fight for honours in taking care of Mum.'

If the poor woman left the table alive, he added in bleak silence as he strode out of the room, grateful that Dani seemed to have everything so well organised, and automatically began to scrub at the deep stainless steel sink.

The list of obvious injuries the woman had sustained was impressive, including complex breaks to both legs and a fractured pelvis, but it was the fact that her blood pressure was plummeting in spite of the enormous amounts of fluid they were pumping into her that was causing most concern. With four major blood vessels in the pelvis, it was becoming increasingly likely that at least one of them had significant damage and was haemorrhaging vast quantities that could only be stemmed when her baby was out of the way.

'That's if it isn't a placental abruption that's causing the blood loss,' he muttered just as Dani joined him at the sink.

'There isn't any evidence of blood loss to indicate that it's the pregnancy that's causing the problem,' she said firmly, almost as if she'd been reading his mind while he'd contemplated the alternatives. 'That means that if it *is* placental abruption, the bleeding's completely contained within the uterus, therefore the intrauterine pressure should be counteracting it to a certain extent.'

She leant forward to use her elbow on the long-lever tap and brushed against his side, sending a shower of sparks right through him and setting every hormone on alert.

'With all those fractures,' she continued, apparently totally unaware of the chaos she was causing to his breathing and blood pressure, 'it's far more likely to be one of the pelvic blood vessels so you need to get that baby out of there, pronto.'

'Well, let's get going, then,' he snapped, strangely angry that she obviously wasn't equally affected by his proximity.

She was almost on his heels as he stepped up to the scrub nurse holding out the green cotton gown for him, waiting for him to thrust his arms into the stiff, crumpled-looking sleeves, and she was right at his shoulder when he stepped up to the side of the operating table.

'Is everybody ready?' he demanded as the operating field was prepped, concentrating on the clock inside his head that told him the woman's time was growing shorter with every tick rather than on the clean soapy scent of Dani's skin that never seemed to be completely covered by the antiseptic smell.

One part of him wanted to do the most direct incision possible to remove the infant as quickly as he could from the one place that should have been a safe refuge. The other part of him knew that, should the mother survive, it would add insult to injury if she lost her baby and was unable to carry another because of his precipitate cutting.

'Suction,' he muttered, sending up a brief prayer of thanks as nothing more than amniotic fluid gushed out of the incision. There was no evidence of bleeding into the uterus and the placenta was positioned well out of the way of the incision. He paused just long enough for suction to clear his field before he motioned the instrument away and enlarged the opening.

'May I?' Dani asked as he set aside the scalpel, and when he nodded she reached slender hands into the opening and emerged within seconds cradling a slippery head no bigger than an orange. 'Have you got the clamps ready?' she asked as she slid her second hand deeper, and he knew that she would be trying to support the weight of the baby's body...not that it would weigh a great deal at this many weeks gestation. 'Could you position them as close to the placenta as practicable, then allow the placental blood to drain down into the baby?' she suggested, and he was glad that his mask covered his expression when a quick grin tugged at the corner of his mouth.

They'd had a conversation about this topic only the other day, debating the benefits to newborns of taking the time to top up their tiny systems with as much blood as possible.

'So what if it means the placenta and cord end up in two separate pieces?' she'd argued. 'Really tiny babies need every bit of blood they can hang onto, so what does it matter if you separate the cord from the placenta in the mother then cut it again closer to the baby when the blood's had a chance to drain down?'

The fact that he'd been doing just that in nearly every delivery for some time wasn't something he'd bothered to tell her. He'd been enjoying himself far too much listening to her fighting her corner.

'And what if the cord blood is needed for other purposes?' he'd argued, purely for argument's sake. 'Researchers are crying out for it for everything from investigations into genetically inherited diseases to ways of persuading bodies to repair their own degenerative conditions.'

'And there are enough full-term healthy babies being born who could spare those last drops of blood,' she said with a fervent light in her eyes. 'Our preemies need it for themselves.'

So, in spite of the fact that it was a more awkward process than immediately cutting the cord close to the baby's belly, he deliberately positioned the clamps as far away as possible.

He glanced up briefly, raising one questioning eyebrow as he met those deep blue eyes over the stark white of her disposable mask and was strangely warmed by the way her eyes gleamed back at him with the evidence of an answering smile.

'Are you ready for me to start injecting dye?' asked a voice on the other side of the table, and it took a second or two before he could work out what the man was talking about.

'And for me to get some X-rays taken,' added another.

'Go ahead,' he invited, knowing that the sooner they worked out how many bleeding blood vessels they were dealing with, and how severe the fractures were, the better for their patient's prognosis. 'Can you work around me while I finish getting the placenta out?'

The rest of his part of the job would almost have been routine if it hadn't been for the air of urgency that permeated the room. And it wasn't just the fact that the monitors were shrilling out warnings every few seconds as the young woman's pulse rate raced and her blood pressure dropped lower and lower.

Behind him there was an ominous absence of sound from the tiny being that Dani had lifted so competently from its mother's womb; just the muttered imprecations between midwife and paediatrician while they exhorted the immature lungs to take that first all-important breath.

That first weak, scratchy cry sounded more like a kitten's mew and coincided exactly with the vascular surgeon's exclamation of relief that he'd found the damaged artery.

'Gotcha!' he gloated just as Josh finally inserted the last suture in the empty uterus and stepped back from the table.

'I'll leave her in your hands,' he said as he stripped off his blood-soaked clothing and prepared to follow the humidicrib to his domain, strangely reluctant to leave the young woman until he knew her fate. But there was nothing further he could do for her—her life was in the hands of other specialists. He needed to concentrate on doing everything he could to make certain that, should she come through this, she would have a healthy baby waiting to greet her.

CHAPTER FOUR

'THERE'S something wrong with her breathing,' Dani snapped before they'd even positioned the humidicrib and connected all the travelling leads to the unit's central monitoring system.

Josh flicked the last switch and the cacophony of bleeps and alarms agreed with her, but he hadn't needed any of them to tell him that his newest charge was in serious trouble.

'She's having to fight for every breath,' Dani muttered as she double-checked the oxygen supply. 'Do you think she's going to need surfactant in her lungs to stop the surfaces sticking?'

He watched the way those tiny ribs were trying to drag air in, and knew from far too much experience that it wasn't a good sign. Such a tiny body just wouldn't have enough reserves of strength to keep the muscles working at that pitch for very long, and a shortage of oxygen spelled certain disaster for all the baby's other systems. The last thing this little scrap needed was brain damage and cardiac arrest.

Unfortunately, there had been no chance to administer corticosteroids to the mother prior to delivery, and as the baby still had some way to go to reach thirty-four weeks, the lungs hadn't developed far enough to produce their own natural surfactant.

'There's a greater risk of brain haemorrhage if she's struggling like this, isn't there? Can't we just raise the pressure of the oxygen a bit to help her?' The concern on Dani's face was as acute as if the tiny girl had been her own, and that once more raised warning flags in Josh's mind.

But it was early days yet, he reminded himself. She'd only been on the unit a matter of days, so there was time for her to learn to distance herself just a little bit, for the sake of her own emotional health.

'Ordinarily, yes, we could, but with respiratory

distress syndrome, if we increase the oxygen pressure to help expand the lungs, we risk rupturing the tissues because they are still so stiff that they can't stretch and move properly,' he reminded her, even as he made a silent note to keep an eye on his newest member of staff. The last thing she needed in her first week on the unit was to get too involved with a baby who had so little chance of survival.

If he could make sure that she had as little to do with this patient as possible…

'And she doesn't need a pneumothorax on top of everything else,' Dani agreed grimly, and he was aware that she was watching his every move as he, in turn, double-checked the settings of every piece of equipment.

'We've done everything we can for the moment.' He risked a glance in her direction and saw the worried pleat between her brows. 'Dani, to a certain extent the babies have to do the work for themselves. Much of what we do is managing the situation from day to day or, during a crisis, from minute to minute. But we can't do it all. The baby's body has to fight to survive, too, and some of them just don't seem to want to do that. That's why there's always a—'

'Josh? Can you come and put a new line in?' called a voice from the other side of the unit just as one of the monitors beside him shrilled out another warning.

Momentarily dragged in two directions at once, he suddenly realised that this would be a good moment to let Dani fly solo.

'Are you happy to put a line in?' he asked, and saw the brief flash of terror in her eyes that was swiftly replaced by pleasure that he'd asked her to do it, mixed with the determination to make a good job of it.

He sighed softly as she made her way across the room, dragging his covetous gaze away from hips that were surprisingly curvaceous for one so small and forcing himself to focus on the detached sensor that had been the cause of the malfunction.

Dani had always been easy to read, right from her childhood, every emotion showing so clearly in her face that it was impossible for her to tell a lie.

She would probably be horrified to know that he'd been able to tell just how delighted she was to be offered the chance to put that line in without having him breathing down her neck. Not that she should have been surprised. He already knew that she had good technique and that, unless there was a problem, there was no reason why she shouldn't be able to make a good job of it. After all, she'd managed to do a similar one on her very first day when her nerves must have been at their jumpiest.

No, he didn't have a problem with her skills as a doctor. His doubts about having her choose this specialty were probably a combination of brotherly concern that she might find the emotional burden of dealing with this environment too stressful and pure selfishness. What else could he call it when it was his own problem with working in the same unit with her that was prompting him to suggest she choose another discipline?

As it was, he was going to have less than six months to prepare himself for the eventuality that, by the time she finished her rotation, she could choose to apply for a permanent post in the unit. If that happened, he was going to have to find some way of giving her the recommendation she deserved for a job in another unit without having to admit why he wasn't willing to appoint her to his own. That was a tightrope he hoped he'd never have to walk.

Of course, if the next weeks and months were particularly harrowing, she might make her own decision not to stay, but from the expression on her face as she straightened up from success-fully threading a hair-fine needle into a vein not much bigger, that wasn't going to be happening any time soon.

As if she'd felt him watching her, Dani glanced up and met his gaze head on, her blue eyes alight with a blaze of triumph, her whole face wreathed in a smile that was visible even behind the dis-posable mask.

A tap on the window caught his attention and the speculative expression on Caitlin's face as she beckoned him across told him she'd caught that exchange of smiles with Dani.

Damn! he thought as he felt a very adolescent blush wash up over his face. The last thing either of them needed was to be the subject of hospital gossip. As it was, only the other members of the interviewing board knew that he'd exempted himself from her interview, and even they didn't know the full details of the relationship between the two of them.

'Sorry to interrupt,' Caitlin said slyly when he stuck his head out of the door. 'But I thought you'd want an update.'

'Update?' He honestly hadn't a clue what his highly efficient secretary was talking about.

'On the RTA mum you left in surgery?' she prompted, and he could have kicked himself. Ordinarily, he would have remembered to check intermittently to see how the mother of one of his patients was doing…and Caitlin knew it. It was another strike against him that, with Dani in the unit, he'd completely forgotten about the poor woman he'd left on the operating table hovering between life and death.

'Tell me the worst,' he invited, wishing he

hadn't dragged his disposable mask off to dangle against his throat. He could have done with something to hide behind with this woman watching his every move.

'They're still trying to get her blood pressure up off the floor, but at least she's not losing any more. Orthopaedics and Vascular are now arguing over whether she's strong enough to start some of the pinning and plating to put her back together or whether to wait and take her up to Theatre again tomorrow or the next day, when she's stronger.'

'If I were a betting man, I'd put money on Orthopaedics winning that round,' he said. 'There's some major long-bone involvement there, as well as the instability caused by the pelvic fracture. If her body's going to be fighting, I would have thought that it might just as well be fighting to repair things when they're all back in roughly the right places. Anyway, thanks for the update and let me know who wins the battle in the OR...I'm glad it's not my call.'

As for the battle in his unit, so far it looked as

if Dani was winning *that*, hands down. Where he was distracted beyond anything in his life before, she seemed to be having no trouble keeping her eyes and her mind on what she was supposed to be doing.

'By the way, Josh,' Caitlin called, catching him looking at Dani again, 'you haven't forgotten that your outpatients clinic starts in twenty minutes, have you?'

He gave her a dismissive wave to send her on her way but doubted that it would have fooled her.

Of course he'd forgotten about the clinic, and if he was being charitable to himself, he could excuse the fact on the grounds that he'd had that RTA delivery to do, but it wouldn't be the truth. He didn't have to look any further than the other side of the room, to the petite woman talking earnestly to a pair of tearful parents, to know where his concentration had gone.

'I'm exhausted!' Dani groaned aloud as she slumped back onto her bed, too tired even to swing her feet up from the floor.

The gentle tap at the door was unexpected. She'd barely caught sight of her new neighbours in the last couple of days, let alone had a conversation with them. She certainly hadn't made any friends who might call round.

'Josh?' she whispered, and suddenly found the energy to leap off the bed and drag frantic fingers through her hair.

'Coming,' she called, and the door swung open to reveal several smiling faces.

'You did say "Come in", didn't you?' the tallest of the group asked as they trooped into her room bearing an assortment of plates, glasses and bottles. 'Well, it doesn't really matter as we're in now,' she continued, making a bee-line for the desk and unceremoniously shoving aside Dani's meticulously organised study notes to unload her burden.

'Hope you like Thai,' said another of the invaders with a smile as she held up a couple of carriers. 'We got a complete selection, so there should be something you like.'

'Yes, but...' Dani might as well have tried to

stop the wind blowing or a river flowing as stop this group from taking over her meagre space. At least the lively invasion had prevented her from feeling more than the first pang that it hadn't been Josh coming to visit.

'We would have been over on the day you moved in, but we couldn't get ourselves organised in time, so this is your official welcome party.'

'And it's a perfect excuse not to do anything this evening other than eat, drink and gossip. Here, grab a plate and get stuck in before the rest of these gannets start eating,' the tallest of the group instructed. 'By the way, I'm Lucinda, or Luce for short, and I've just started a six-month rotation on Orthopaedics.' She pulled a face as she brushed unruly dark hair back over her shoulder. 'There's far too much hammer and chisel work involved for my taste, apart from the fact I'm working with Neanderthals. Did you know the rumours are all true? Their knuckles *do* scrape along the ground as they walk!'

'Oh, Luce, you're dreadful! You're only miffed because there aren't any hunky sportsmen around—rugby-playing doctors or injured patients. I'm Magda, by the way,' said the elegant young woman with the perfect dark bob. 'I've just started on Paeds too, I've seen you in Neonatal. Don't you think Mr Weatherby is just the most gorgeous—?'

'Oh, give it a rest, Magda. You'll be getting dirty rabbits on your tongue if it hangs out any further. Still, all the while you're talking you're not eating, so there's more for the rest of us,' said the third member of the group in a heavily accented voice. 'I'm Tomasz,' he announced with a cheeky smile and a flash of bright blue eyes between sooty lashes. 'I'm working in A and E and I'm far handsomer than Mr Icy Weatherman because I'm available.'

'In your dreams!'

'No chance!' hooted the others.

'And the phrase you *should* have used is "dust bunnies", not "dirty rabbits",' instructed the last member of the group in a soft Irish accent. She was at least ten years older than the rest and had the heavily freckled skin that went with her carroty curls. 'I'm Marion and I'm only included in these feasts on sufferance because I'm not one of you lofty doctor types. I'm only here doing a three-month midwifery refresher. Can I pour you some wine? We only got white, I'm afraid, and it's nothing marvellous. Strictly cheap and cheerful.'

'Is there any other sort?' Dani asked with a smile as she accepted a tumbler full of pale straw-coloured liquid. She wasn't quite sure what to do with it because her other hand was already holding a plate full of steaming aromatic food and there wasn't a single inch of space free to put anything down.

Still, she wasn't complaining. This was the sort of welcome she'd never dreamed of when she'd applied for the job. All too often, progress up through the ranks in a medical career meant up-rooting yourself at regular intervals as you went on to a new post to take you up to the next rung, and leaving all your friends behind.

'So, tell us everything,' Luce said when they were all settled, some sitting on furniture while the unlucky ones sprawled on the floor with food and drinks balanced wherever they could find space.

'Yes,' agreed Phyl. 'Who did you have to kill—?'

'Or sleep with?' Marion interjected with an eyebrow-waggling grin.

'To get a job with Mr Drop-Dead-Gorgeous?' Luce finished.

'Ah, please!' Tomasz complained. 'Dani is as beautiful as a little doll but *he* is not so good-looking. He is not even tall and dark as I am. He is more like a lion while I...*I* am the sexy panther.' His eyebrow-waggling was accompanied with a definite leer, but Dani couldn't really have cared.

Was *Josh* the reason for this show of friendship from her new housemates in the staff accommodation block? If so, they were going to be disappointed. They wouldn't be getting any information to feed the gossip mill from her, especially not the fact that she and Josh had been brought up as brother and sister.

'I'm sorry to let you all down, but there weren't

any unexplained deaths involved, or any illicit assignations. In fact, Mr Weatherby wasn't even present at my interview.'

'You mean you actually applied for the job because you *wanted* it and not because it was in Josh Weatherby's department?' Luce didn't sound as if she could believe such a thing.

'Oh, I applied because the vacancy was in his department—'

'Aha! I knew it!' Phyl exclaimed. 'The man is totally irresistible. Those golden eyes make you feel warm right through, and when he smiles…'

'And *that* was because the department has such a good reputation,' Dani continued stubbornly, totally ignoring the interruption, 'and the survival stats for the babies that go through there are the equal of any department in the country—and that's in spite of the fact that they're dealing with some of the most fragile preemies you can get.'

'So…you are unimpressed by the older man,' Tomasz decided, clearly delighted with his deduction. 'You are more impressed with someone closer to your own age, perhaps… someone more available…someone closer to—'

'Oh, Tomasz, give it a rest,' Marion said around a mouthful of aromatic rice. 'You're going to give us all indigestion and we won't invite you to join us again.'

'Don't worry about me, Marion,' Dani reassured her. 'I've had many years of learning how to fend off over-eager medical students. Somehow they always seem to see my lack of height as an indication that I'm childish and naïve, so I'm used to it. Anyway, as a last resort I can always introduce them to my much bigger brother. It's amazing how well they behave once they've seen him,' Especially once they realised that an adverse comment about harrassment from her-big-brother-the-consultant could do their careers a lot of harm. 'He taught me to fight dirty, too,' she added wickedly, with a pointed glance from her knee to his crotch.

Tomasz looked predictably pained at the thought and the three women burst into laughter at his suddenly renewed interest in his food.

'Well, *I* think it's a waste of an opportunity,' Luce mourned as she went back to the containers of food for a second helping. 'You're going to be working with him every day and he's single, gainfully employed, heterosexual and gorgeous and you're not interested in marrying him.'

Dani wouldn't go quite that far. If Josh ever fell in love with her in any other than a brotherly way, she'd marry him so fast it would make everybody's head spin. But that was about as likely as...well, as likely as her finally putting on a growth spurt and getting those model's legs she'd always wanted.

'What can I tell you?' Dani said with a shrug, grateful that the light on her side of the room was subdued enough to hide the wash of heat that had flooded through her at the thought of marrying Josh—as if *that* was ever going to happen. 'I'm only going to be working with him for six months and I've got an awful lot to learn before I can take my next lot of exams. I certainly won't have time to chase him around the department, trying to get a ring on my finger.'

'But it might have been fun,' Marion teased,

and her brogue made the idea seem even more enticing somehow.

Perhaps that was why, once her room was her own again and she was tucked up under the covers, trying to sleep, all she could think about was chasing Josh around the department until he gave in and finally finished the kiss she'd started the night of her eighteenth birthday.

The images must have followed her into her dreams because she woke up the next morning with her pulse racing, the bedclothes twisted around her body and a dreadful empty feeling around her heart with the realisation that none of her wild imaginings ever had a chance of coming true.

Then she arrived on the unit and the first person she saw was Josh, emerging from the staff cloakroom, looking as if he'd only just woken up. Lust struck her hard and fast when she took in the rumpled hair and crumpled shirt and imagined waking up beside him and seeing him looking exactly like that. But even as she battled to stop herself from drooling, a deeper emotion wrapped itself around her heart when she saw how exhausted he looked.

'Another long night?' she asked, trying not to notice that he still dragged the fingers of both hands through his hair, the way he always had first thing in the morning, right from her earliest memories.

'Very long. If it wasn't one of them going through a crisis, it was another,' he sighed. 'I'll go through it all with you at the morning meeting.'

'Would a coffee help?'

'The stronger the better, and preferably delivered intravenously,' he said wearily. 'Unfortunately, I've got some surgical procedures to do this morning.'

'And the caffeine might induce a hand tremor,' she finished for him. 'I'll find something else. Where will you be?'

'In my office. I need to change my shirt then I'll be making a start on some of the interminable paperwork, for my sins.' He briefly pulled a wry face then smiled at her, giving her just a glimpse of a dimple as she turned away, hoping he hadn't read her reaction to the idea that he was going to be stripping his shirt off in his office.

'Dani?' he called after her, and she looked over her shoulder to find him leaning back tiredly against the doorframe. 'You do know you don't *have* to do this? It's not part of your duties as newest member of the team.'

'You didn't ask. I offered,' she pointed out, wondering what he'd say if she were to tell him how much more she'd be willing to do for him. Probably run screaming in the other direction.

She was glad she'd decided to come in to work early because that meant the café run by the league of volunteers wasn't trying to cope with the sudden influx of staff going off duty when she arrived. Even so, it was close to fifteen minutes before she tapped in the access code at the entrance to the unit.

'I come bearing gifts,' she announced as she carefully balanced the laden tray one-handed to tap and open his office door...and nearly dropped the lot when she found him standing in the middle of the room naked to the waist, his arms raised as he vigorously towelled his hair.

Only lightning-fast reflexes enabled her to

maintain her hold on the tray, but even then some of the grapefruit juice slopped over the top of the glass and the pile of toast slid dangerously close to the edge of the plate. Meanwhile, she was taking full advantage of the fact that he hadn't realised she was there, her eyes travelling greedily over the expanse of golden-brown skin stretched tautly over flat slabs of muscles across his chest and a prominently ribbed six-pack leading down to his lean waist.

Where had all those muscles come from, and when? They certainly hadn't been there when he'd taken her swimming in the summers during his medical training…or perhaps she just hadn't noticed them then.

Well, they were there now, and how! And so was the tawny silk that stretched in a swirling band right across from one tightly furled male nipple to the other. And his skin… It looked as if it would feel like the most expensive satin and the colour reminded her of butterscotch and fudge. As for the stray rivulets of water that purled their way down over the swells and hollows, she could imagine all to easily what it would be like to chase them with her tongue, following them all the way down to—

'Dani! I didn't hear you come in!' Josh exclaimed, dragging her guilty gaze up to meet his. She was amazed to see more than a hint of colour darken the lean planes of his face and realised for the very first time that he might not be quite as immune to her as she'd always thought.

Or was it the sort of reaction that any man would have when he caught a woman ogling him? She really didn't have enough experience to know because, apart from some purely platonic friendships that had developed during her training, she'd never really been interested in anyone other than Josh.

He gave the errant water droplets a cursory swipe with the towel before reaching for his shirt. 'I'll…uh…just get this on,' he said, his voice strangely husky. 'I thought dunking my head under the tap would wake me up a bit.'

More food for thought, Dani mused, her pulse giving a strange little skip when she realised that he didn't seem to want to meet her eyes…and he'd left his shirt uncharacteristically untucked.

'Where shall I put this?' she asked, suddenly realising that she was still standing there with a laden tray in her hands. 'I got grapefruit juice, a pile of toast and a large mug of tea.'

'Is there anything to go on the toast?' He was just doing up the last button on the shirt, completely hiding that mouth-watering body under a professional façade. But she knew it was there now. She'd seen it in all its glory and… What had he asked?

'You think I could live with you for all those years and not know that the only thing you want on your toast in the morning is Seville orange marmalade?' She'd grabbed several miniature pots, knowing he liked the slightly bitter tang far more than sickly sweet jams for breakfast. 'Shall I spread it for you?' she offered, then cringed, only realising just how domestic the conversation sounded when the words were out of her mouth.

'Aren't you having any?' he asked round the first eager mouthful. 'It looks as if you got plenty.'

'I'll just stick to the tea. I had something to eat before I came to work.'

'Don't tell me. You had a big bowl of porridge, even though it's the middle of summer,' he teased.

'Don't you mock my porridge. It's the ideal way to fuel yourself for a busy morning, and that's what I would have eaten if the kitchen over in the staff residency hadn't been left in such a state last night. I really didn't fancy cleaning up a mess on an empty stomach, especially when none of it was mine.'

'You've moved in there?' He seemed surprised. 'Why didn't you find yourself a studio flat or something?'

'It didn't really seem worth all the effort of hunting for one when I'll be moving on in six months. I asked around and was told that the chance of finding anything affordable within easy reach of the hospital is negligible. Anyway,' she said defensively, 'the staff accommodation isn't that bad and it's within walking distance, so it even saves me the expense of travel.'

'That's all very well, but I can remember all too

clearly how noisy they can be. You're never going to be able to get any study done.'

'I'll manage somehow,' she said firmly, knowing that she was probably sticking her chin out at what he'd always called a combative angle. 'I'm not going to let a bit of noise set me off course at this late stage.'

'Don't bite my head off.' He held up both hands. 'I was only concerned that it might be too much to cope with on top of a stressful job. Anyway, it's something to think about. And if you get stuck and it's not working out where you are, you could always move into my spare room.'

The expression on his face told her that he was almost as shocked that he'd made the offer as she was to hear it, especially in view of the way he'd been steering clear of her as much as he could in the department.

'I'm sure that won't be necessary,' she said hastily, and he immediately looked so relieved that her pride was piqued. He should know that, no matter how awkward it might be, profession-ally, to have her under his roof, she wouldn't be a bad housemate. They had both been taught to pick up after themselves by the same mother after all.

Her obstinate streak put in an unexpected appearance and she heard herself adding airily, 'But I'll keep your offer in mind, thank you, just in case the study situation *does* become impossible.'

It was only much later that she realised that she might have had a deeper subconscious reason for making sure that his offer hadn't been completely turned down; that she had actually left herself with a good solid excuse to move in with the man who filled her thoughts nearly every hour of her day and an increasing number of her dreams. But if she were to move in with him so that they were sharing his personal space, too…well, wouldn't the hospital gossips have a field day with *that*?

CHAPTER FIVE

A WEEK later Josh's offer was seeming more attractive by the minute.

Tonight the whole building seemed to be pulsating with the incessant beat of the music that was pounding in the common room on the ground floor.

'Don't be a spoilsport,' she muttered to herself, and flopped back in her seat to gaze unseeingly at the books and papers spread out on the desk in front of her. She'd been trying to study for more than an hour now, and doubted that she'd taken in a single thing.

'It's a birthday party, that's all,' she reminded herself, wondering if she would have done better to accept the invitation Natasha had slipped under her door a couple of days ago. But she'd never really been a party person, especially when she didn't really know any of the other people there.

Then there was the fact that she hadn't been in the mood for a party, anyway…not after the sad events in the unit today.

The twins would have been the perfect family for Clive and Joanna Rushworth, a couple who'd been forced to wait for fifteen years before her domineering parents had finally died and they had been free to marry.

'We thought we were making up for lost time when we were told it was twins,' Joanna had confided tearfully as she sat between the two isolettes, watching her two tiny sons fight the unequal battle for survival. 'My mother was an invalid and my father wouldn't allow anyone else into the house to care for her. Then, when she died, he insisted that it was my duty to continue to keep house for him as he'd supported me all my life.'

'And Clive waited for you all that time?' Dani marvelled.

'He said he didn't want anyone else,' Joanna

said shyly. 'Even though my father did everything he could to frighten him away, Clive always found a way of letting me know that he was there.' There was a mischievous edge to her smile. 'We'll always be glad for the invention of the Internet.'

'Was that how you kept in touch?' Dani was intrigued. She couldn't imagine that there were many couples who had to travel such a long rocky road to matrimony.

'Once we realised that my father was destroying any letter Clive tried to send.' She chuckled. 'He phoned, posing as a telephone salesman, to tell me that I'd won a computer in a competition, then he paid for someone to deliver it and set it up for me. Father would have refused to let me buy one, but he wasn't likely to turn down something that was apparently free.

'After that, it was easy to send messages backwards and forwards whenever we had the chance, and to plan for the future, once Mother no longer needed me. We never dreamed it would be more than fifteen years before we could really be together, and when I fell pregnant on our honeymoon…'

Every conversation was bound to come back to the misery of the present day. It seemed as if this poor couple had been granted such a short measure of happiness.

'Did you have no idea that there was anything wrong with the babies?' As long as there was nothing urgent demanding her attention on the unit, Dani didn't mind keeping Joanna company until Clive returned. She could always catch up on her share of the paperwork later—after all, it was unlikely to be very long before this sad episode came to its inevitable conclusion.

'When I had the scan, they said that one baby was bigger than the other, but no one seemed particularly concerned. Then we had the chance to go away for a little holiday together, to a villa owned by a friend.' Her smile spoke of happy memories. 'Apart from our week's honeymoon in Venice, it was the first time I'd ever been abroad on holiday. My first time swimming in an outdoor pool with wall-to-wall sunshine; my first time wandering around a market, choosing all the exotic things to eat that I'd never even tasted before; my first time feeling as if I was just the same as everybody else.'

There was an apologetic look on her face as she hastened to add, 'I made sure to speak to my midwife to tell her what we wanted to do, and even though I had a second scan booked for the time we were away, she told us to go and have a wonderful time.'

'And was it wonderful?' Dani hardly needed to ask. The blush on Joanna's face was enough to make her jealous.

'I'd never even had a tan before,' she said, then leant towards Dani and beckoned her closer to whisper, 'And certainly not one without any strap marks…anywhere!'

'Good for you! That's something I've never dared to do,' Dani admitted, then blushed equally fiercely when a sudden picture leapt into her head of lying naked under a warm foreign sun while skilful male hands smoothed oil over her limbs, careful to make sure that it was spread to every hidden crevice. She didn't need to see the man's face to know whose hands they were, neither did she doubt that she would be equally as assiduous when she returned the favour.

'Then we came home and went to the rescheduled scan and they told us that there was something wrong with the babies' circulation—that one of them was being starved of blood and that the other one's system was so overloaded that it was damaging his heart.'

Dani had been trying to read about the clinical management of such situations this evening, wanting to understand exactly what had gone wrong with Joanna's pregnancy and what else could have been done to rectify it.

Unfortunately, despite Joanna's own specialist's expertise in the field, labour had been precipitated by an attempt at *in utero* surgery, and the desperately premature babies had been rushed to Josh's unit in the vain hope that he might be able to work a miracle.

Should the surgeon have waited and watched for a few more days or weeks until the babies' gestational age gave them a better chance at survival? Had the steroids done all they could to mature the lungs? If surgery had been imperative at that stage, could stronger drugs have prevented Joanna going into labour for those vital extra days?

There always seemed to be more questions than answers, which was a very scary thought when it wouldn't be long before she was supposed to be the one coming up with those answers.

'And I'm never going to be able to get all that information into my head if I can't even hear myself think,' she growled aloud, and threw her hands up in the air.

Her phone rang at that moment and she nearly screamed with frustration at yet another interruption.

She hadn't been blessed with Josh's phenomenal memory. She had to study really hard for every exam, and just at the moment it seemed as if everything was against her.

'What?' she snapped into the receiver, then felt

dreadful when she heard her adoptive mother's concerned voice on the other end.

'Have I called at a bad time, love?' she asked. 'You're not still on duty, are you? I thought this was your evening off.'

'It is, Mum, and I'm sorry for snapping, but…well, I've been trying to do some study and there's a birthday party going on downstairs.'

'Josh said he was worried that you might have a few problems living there,' she said. 'There have always been a few medical students who can't party in moderation.'

'Unlike your new husband,' Dani teased, quickly changing the subject to something far more pleasant. 'How's married life with the most patient man on the planet?'

'I would thoroughly recommend it,' Meredith Kasarian said with laughter in her voice.

In the background Dani could hear the murmur of the retired consultant's voice and was delighted all over again that he'd finally persuaded his senior nurse to accept his proposal. They both deserved some happiness, Meredith after being alone for so many years, struggling to bring up two children single-handedly, and Kas after nursing his wife until cancer had finally taken her life. Josh and Dani hadn't been the only ones who had cheered when the two long-time colleagues had announced their engagement.

'So, apart from the difficulties of finding somewhere quiet enough to study, how's the new job going?' Meredith prompted. 'No regrets about applying for the post on Josh's team? You know you would have been welcomed with open arms in my old department.'

'I know, Mum, but I decided I'd rather make my mistakes somewhere that the whole of the staff didn't know everything about me from when I drew my first breath. At least in Josh's unit I'm anonymous, just another trainee doing her six months.'

'Hardly "just another trainee" when your big brother is the boss,' Meredith pointed out with a laugh. 'I hope that isn't causing any problems.'

Dani paused momentarily, hoping Meredith would understand.

'Nobody knows,' she admitted.

'Nobody knows what?' Meredith's puzzlement was clear even from half a world away.

'About Josh and me… It wasn't done deliberately,' she added hurriedly. 'But when it was obvious that none of the rest of his staff knew there was any connection, it seemed simpler not to say anything.' Especially as Josh seemed to want it that way. Then there was the fact that she hadn't really felt as if Josh was her brother for a long time now. Unfortunately, there seemed to be little chance that he would see her as something other than his little sister.

'I don't understand,' the voice in the distance said plaintively. 'I always thought you were so proud of your big brother. You used to follow him around, right from the day you took your first steps.'

Damn. This was just what she didn't want— for Meredith to be upset that things couldn't always go on the way they had when she herself had been a little girl. But she wasn't a little girl any more. She was a woman making her way in a demanding profession and she—

A sudden knock at the door gave her the ideal chance to end the uncomfortable conversation before she managed to put her foot in her mouth.

'I'm sorry, Mum, I've got to go. There's someone at the door. Have a wonderful time and give Kas a big hug for me.'

'I'll hang on a moment just in case it's Josh,' she said. 'I've been trying to ring him for several days but he's never home.'

Dani knew exactly how little time he'd spent away from the unit. She hadn't seen him connected to the Internet once, even though she'd been longing for a 'conversation' with him.

'We've had several very poorly babies and you know what he's like…doesn't like to leave them if there's a chance they may need him.'

The knock came again, firm enough to be male knuckles, and she hoped it wasn't Tomasz hoping to persuade her to join the party. She'd already turned him down twice. Still, holding a phone to her ear would be a good excuse for turning him down yet again.

It *was* Tomasz and she was delighted to be able

to tell him she was talking to her mother before shutting him firmly on the other side of the door.

'Are you sure you didn't want to go out with that young man?' Meredith asked, and even over thousands of miles Dani could hear a hint of the newlywed's euphoria that made her mother wish for the same happiness for her.

'Mum, even if I was interested in him, I wouldn't want to go down to that party with him. The music's turned up so loud that I can barely hear myself think, and I'm another two stories further up.'

'Well, don't you go sticking your nose in a study book all the time or all the nice young men will be gone, and then where will you be?' Meredith fretted.

'I'll have both my feet firmly planted on the career ladder, doing a job I love,' Dani told her, even though she knew it wouldn't deflect her from a complaint that was coming more and more frequently as the years flew past.

'You and Josh are far too alike in that,' Meredith continued, almost as if Dani hadn't spoken. 'Neither of you look as if you'll be settling down any time soon, and while Kaz's grandchildren are beautiful, I'm looking forward to holding some of my own.'

'Love you, Mum, but I'm afraid you're going to be waiting a bit longer yet. I'll tell Josh you've been trying to get hold of him.'

'OK, well, give him a hug for me. Love you, Dani,' Meredith said, ringing off.

The phone call was over but that didn't mean she could study, and this time she couldn't even blame the intrusive music. All she could think about was the fact that the phone call had only been the second time in her life that Dani had deliberately avoided telling Meredith what she was really feeling.

The first time had been when she'd been a teenager, struggling with her changing feelings for the big brother she'd always idolised. Everything inside her had been so complicated and so overwhelming that she just wouldn't have been able to put it all into words. It had seemed scary and exciting all at the same time, and when she'd made up her mind that her eighteenth birthday—the day she would officially be recognised as an adult—was going to be the day that she told Josh how she felt about him… For those few days, it had been like hugging the best secret in the world.

Of course, in her naïveté she'd convinced herself that Josh felt the same about her, and was only waiting until her birthday to declare himself, too.

She'd been so glad that she'd never told Meredith about it—that humiliation on top of his horrified rejection would have been too much to bear.

This time she was under no illusions that he felt the same way she did. The first time she'd caught sight of him in the unit had told her that her feelings for him hadn't faded with time and distance—unfortunately.

His emotions were another matter entirely.

It went without saying that he cared about her, but, then, that had been the case before she'd even been born. No, the thing that had really stung was that in this new role he obviously intended treating her with thoroughly professional detachment and that, as she had discovered over the last few days, was almost worse. She wanted...*needed* more from him than brotherly concern but didn't think she would ever be lucky enough to get it, especially as now he clearly saw her as nothing more than the newest junior member of staff in his unit.

She sighed at the tangled emotions inside her, knowing exactly why she hadn't said anything to Meredith. It just wouldn't have felt right to offload her frustrations about her situation with Josh onto someone who was supposed to be on her honeymoon, let alone the fact that she was the mother of the man who had her permanently hot and bothered.

There was another knock at her door and she groaned aloud, secure in the knowledge that she couldn't be heard outside in the noisy corridor.

'When *will* he get the message?' she muttered through gritted teeth, and picked the phone up again as she strode across to the door, fully intending to use a non-existent call to put the persistent man off yet again.

Then she pulled the door open and found Josh leaning against the wall outside her room.

'Are you ready to admit that I was right?' he asked, his tone far too smug for Dani's liking.

'Right about what?' she asked wide-eyed, although the music seemed to be louder than ever out here in the corridor.

His wry glance over his shoulder towards the source of the incessant rhythmic thumping said everything without a word being spoken.

'Have you eaten?' he asked, as though such conversations were commonplace between them. 'I need to unwind after…after taking care of all the paperwork.'

'About the twins?' she asked with a heavy heart. Although everyone had hoped that there might be a miracle, they'd all known that there was little chance that the babies would survive for very long. It had been almost a relief when first one and then the other had stopped breathing, and Dani had felt so guilty for feeling that way. 'How are the parents?'

'Devastated. Inconsolable. Blaming themselves and trying to work out what they did wrong that made this happen.' He shook his head. 'I know we aren't supposed to let it get to us, but it wrings me out every time. Will you keep me company so I can switch off from it?'

For several seconds the invitation robbed her of speech, especially as he'd been so distant ever since she'd joined his team. Not that she would ever turn down the chance to spend time in his company.

'How can I refuse, especially when the alternative is trying to study with all that noise going on?' She stepped back to let him come into the room, suddenly filled with a bubbling sense of excitement. She'd just spent a large part of the day working in the same department with the man and she couldn't wait to be in his company again, and if that wasn't crazy, nothing was. 'I'll just grab a jacket and my purse.'

He leant one shoulder against the doorframe and pulled a face as he looked around the room. 'These places are even worse than I remembered. I've seen bigger rabbit hutches.'

'Don't. You'll depress me even further.' She

tucked her phone in her jacket pocket with her keys and suddenly remembered Meredith's call. 'By the way, the honeymooners rang a little earlier. They said they'd been trying to catch you for a few days but you're never home.' She wondered whether she'd have the nerve to deliver the hug Meredith had sent and her pulse jumped for several seconds at the thought of having her arms around Josh after nine long years.

The last few days she'd almost become accustomed to his occasional nearness and to being surrounded by the mixture of soap and musk and skin that was his alone, but that didn't mean that her heart didn't beat just that bit harder and faster every time she breathed it in. But being in close physical contact the way she would have to be if she were to hug him, that would be something else again.

And if she tried it now, there was every likelihood that she would be eating alone if his reaction was the same as the last time she'd put her arms around him, so that might not be a good idea.

Perhaps later, she thought as she pulled the door shut behind her and checked that the catch had engaged. Perhaps she'd do it after they'd had their meal...before they went their separate ways, he to the quiet serenity of his bachelor flat and she back to the noisy chaos of the staff accommodation block.

Except, while the two of them were sharing an enormous mound of pasta in a little Italian restaurant that was obviously a favourite haunt of Josh's, her brain ceased to function properly. She couldn't even taste the creamy sauce laden with loads of bacon and Parmesan cheese because the only thing she could think about was that this was Josh sitting next to her, of his own choice.

That was Josh's elbow brushing against her own as he battled with a tangle of linguini, his lean powerful thigh just inches away from her leg as they shared a banquette in a secluded alcove.

If this hadn't been Josh, it would have seemed very much like a date, but, then, if it hadn't been Josh, she wouldn't have accepted the invitation, because ever since she'd realised just how deep her feelings were for him, no other man had been able to measure up.

And if he never returned her feelings? What then?

Would she have to resign herself to a life dedicated to her profession or would she be able to school herself to settle for second best so that she could know the joys of motherhood and a family of her own?

She desperately needed to talk to someone, but who? There had only really ever been two people in her life to whom she could pour out her heart, Josh and Meredith, and they were the only two she couldn't turn to now.

She sighed at the tangled emotions inside her, even as she tingled with awareness at the proximity of the man at her side and mourned the fact that he would be for ever out of reach.

'That was a heavy sigh,' Josh commented, jerking her out of her introspection.

Everything inside her clenched when she saw the intent expression in those golden eyes. She could imagine that it was the same look in a lion's eyes when it had a gazelle in its sight—unwavering concentration while it tried to predict which way its next meal would jump.

For just a second she was sorely tempted to tell him what she was thinking. It would be such a relief to pour it all out to the person who had listened, endlessly patient, while she'd prattled on as a child.

But she could just imagine the expression on his face if she told him that every time she saw him, every nerve in her body quivered with the elemental awareness of a female for her chosen mate, and all she could think as he was speaking was that she wanted to feel those lips on hers.

'You're overtired,' he diagnosed with a fierce frown when she was unable to come up with a single word, an alternative topic of conversation completely eluding her. 'You need to get some sleep or you'll be useless to me tomorrow. Let's get you to bed.'

To bed?

The pictures in her head were X-rated and any chance she'd had of getting her thoughts into some logical order went right out of the window.

Honestly, she was as obsessed as any hormone-ravaged teenager over the latest pop singer or

film idol, and it was utterly ridiculous in
someone of twenty-seven. If she wasn't going to
go completely round the bend she needed to get
a life, and preferably one that didn't revolve
around Joshua Weatherby.

It was a good job that the walk back to the staff
block wasn't very long because even the work-
related conversation of the outward journey
seemed beyond her. All she could think, as she
glanced in his direction, was that the evening
light was casting his features almost as a sil-
houette against the sky, and that, as ever, he was
adjusting the length of his stride so that she didn't
have to run to keep up with him.

She was sorely tempted to walk just that little
bit closer so that their arms would brush but lost
her nerve at the last moment, afraid that his
reaction to something so blatant would spoil the
memory of the first real time they'd spent
together in years.

Finally, they reached the driveway leading to the
staff residence and the end of their interlude
together. She already had her keys in her hand and

in just a few seconds he would be leaving her to go back into the continuing noise of the party, alone.

Josh had been determined to deliver Dani safely to her front door in spite of the fact that the whole evening must rate as one of the most excruciating of his life.

No matter how hard he'd tried to concentrate on their surroundings and the taste of the food, all he'd been aware of had been the beautiful woman beside him—the scent of her skin, the soft timbre of her voice, the moonbeam paleness of her silky hair, the brush of her arm against his.

And it didn't matter how often he reminded himself that this was his little sister, his body wasn't listening. It had been the same story ever since he'd come out of his office on that first morning and seen her standing at the reception desk. It hardly mattered that he'd been spending extra hours on the unit, keeping an eye on the state of their most volatile patients, because every time he closed his eyes his subconscious was filled with images, and every one of them was of Dani.

He'd tried to concentrate on the memories of the scrawny little scrap she'd been for those first few months, but his dreams were far more interested in the images of the vivacious, laughing teenager she'd grown into. But it was the newest incarnation that was causing him the most problems, that of the mature, ripe woman who could arouse him with nothing more than the scent of her skin as she walked past him in the corridor.

And yet, knowing this, he'd still invited her to spend time with him while they shared a meal.

He must be mad.

With a heavy sigh of his own, he resigned himself to the prospect of yet another long, cold shower when he returned to his flat.

Finally, Dani stepped up to unlock the door and he felt he could relax his vigilant hold on himself just a little. The evening was almost over. In another couple of seconds she would step inside the door and shut it between them and temptation would be out of reach for a few more hours.

The incessant thump of the music had been moderated slightly in their absence, although it had now been joined by the sounds of rather drunken revelry. He still wasn't completely happy about her living here, but at least he now knew that her room had a sturdy lock on the door, so she should be safe.

'By the way, Mum asked me to deliver this,' she said, turning back towards him so that the light streamed over her face, making her look even more like a perfect porcelain doll than usual.

He was so busy trying not to look at her that he hardly realised what she was doing until she'd wrapped both arms around him, her surprisingly curvaceous little body pressed against his from shoulder to thigh as she hugged him tightly.

CHAPTER SIX

ALL the way back to his flat he was kicking himself for overreacting.

If he'd only kept still and quiet, the contact would have been over in another second or two and she would never have known that his body had responded so strongly.

Well, that wasn't strictly true. His body had reacted to her from the moment he'd had the crazy idea of inviting her out for the meal and he'd been on edge the whole time they'd been together.

It hadn't been so bad while they had been sitting side by side or walking together, but when she'd suddenly plastered herself against him like that, he'd automatically wrapped both arms around her, pulling her closer, and there had been no way she could miss the fact that his body wanted far more than a hug from her.

He groaned out loud, prompting a pimply youth with more than his fair share of facial piercings to snarl belligerently, 'What's your problem, mate?'

Josh almost laughed aloud as he imagined the youngster's reaction if he actually told him about the last nine years' torment.

'Work,' he said succinctly, eliciting a blasé snort.

'Tried it once, didn't like it,' he said with a shrug as he sauntered off. 'Got in the way of me social life.'

'A social life that my taxes are funding,' Josh muttered under his breath, but he was grateful for the fact that the encounter had at least put a stop to his spiralling thoughts.

Now all he had to do was work out what he would say to Dani when he saw her in the morning.

But that was tomorrow. Tonight, he was going to have to try to make contact with his mother and her new husband, if he could work out what the time difference was between them. The last thing he wanted to do was ring when the two of them were in bed.

He pulled a face at the image and wondered how many children felt uncomfortable at the thought of their parents sharing a bed and all the activities that could take place there.

And just that swiftly his head was filled with far more enticing images of Dani in bed…in *his* bed…with her moonbeam-pale hair spread out across his coffee-coloured sheets and her perfectly proportioned little body sprawled in satisfied abandon beside him while they tried to catch their breath.

'Never going to happen,' he reminded himself sternly as he shut the door behind him.

The trouble was, if it wasn't going to happen with Dani, it was beginning to look as if it wasn't going to happen with anyone.

He'd actually got as far as looking at engagement rings with one girlfriend before he'd caught sight of her reflection in the shop window and realised just how much she looked like his little sister. Thank goodness he'd realised in time, because the fact that he must have chosen her purely because his subconscious had picked up on that resemblance could only have spelled disaster for the long-term prospects of the relationship.

But how could he rid himself of something that must surely be bordering on obsession?

The honest answer was that he couldn't, not with his mother still expecting him to keep an eye on Dani.

It might have been different if one or other of them had moved to the other side of the world. Perhaps her image would have had a chance to fade. As it was, he usually spoke to Meredith at least once a week and she was bound to bring up the name of the person who was her daughter in all but blood.

Had he heard from Dani? It was always the first question his mother asked, and for nine years he'd mostly been able to duck any further conversation on that topic with a negative. Now that he and Dani were working in the same department, that was going to be impossible. And his mother was far too intelligent a person not to realise that something was wrong if he stumbled and stammered over what the two of them had been doing together. She would certainly have a few pointed questions if he were to admit that he was actually avoiding being in the same room.

Jake sighed heavily, easily able to imagine the horrified expression on her face if he were to tell her that she was unlikely to get the grandchildren she wanted unless Dani were to produce them.

Then he had to grit his teeth against the murderous rage that surged through him at the thought of someone daring to touch *his* Dani. Everything inside him railed against the idea that she might carry anyone's baby but his, no matter how impossible that was.

Yes, he knew as well as anyone that there was no blood connection between them, and that there was no legal or logical reason why they couldn't marry and have a family, but…

'Apart from anything else, she's far too young for you… or, rather, you're too old for her,' he growled into the emptiness of his smart bachelor bedroom after a phone call to the other side of the world that had gone exactly as he'd predicted.

'So, deal with it and get on with your life,' he instructed himself firmly as he slid into bed, relishing the feel of crisp, smooth sheets against his freshly showered body. 'You'll have hundreds…maybe thousands of babies to take care of during your life, so stop whining about the ones that can never be.'

But speaking sternly to himself didn't mean that he could switch off his dreams and he woke up the next morning with a head full of images that were every bit as explicit as the ones from the night before…and the one before that.

'Pervert!' he muttered to himself as he strode out into the entrance hall of the flats, and the mousy little man who lived on the next floor up dropped his bulky pile of mail and went bright red.

And, of course, Dani was the first person he saw when he keyed open the security door to the unit.

'Good morning, Mr Weatherby,' she called cheerily. 'Did you sleep well?' He could swear that there was a deliberate twinkle in those apparently innocent blue eyes.

'Very well, thank you,' he lied, and after a single all-encompassing glance that took in her form-fitting red-and-white-striped top and her softly draped black trousers he found himself scurrying for his office in need of another cold shower.

'Run, rabbit, run,' Dani murmured with a chuckle as she saw him disappear through the door. But he wasn't going to be able to run very far, neither could he run fast enough, not since her hug last night had shown her the proof that he was physically attracted to her.

'OK, so most men are hard-wired to respond to anything that's female and has a pulse,' she continued softly as she poured boiling water into the teapot and waited impatiently for the tea to infuse to exactly the right colour. But it wasn't just a case of a little sister idolising her big brother that was telling her that Josh wasn't the sort to allow himself to respond to every woman.

In his teens and twenties he'd been so focused

on qualifying for his chosen career that he'd done very little dating at all, and that could only have been through choice. The reaction of her female colleagues was enough to tell her that his present apparent celibacy wasn't through lack of interested women. He was good-looking, intelligent, hard-working, heterosexual and…well, he ticked just about every box for any woman looking for the ideal mate.

He certainly ticked all her boxes in a way that no other man had managed.

'So, today is the day,' she whispered as she picked up two steaming mugs and set off down the corridor. 'No more avoidance, no more sticking my head in the sand and just wishing. From this moment on, I'm going to do everything I can to find out if there's any chance that he feels the same way that I do.'

And if there wasn't…

No! She wasn't even going to think of that possibility, not after that hug had revealed his body's undeniable physiological response to her proximity.

Physiological response. She grinned that such a dry scientific phrase could be used to describe something that had turned her knees to water and sent her pulse and blood pressure rocketing.

That hadn't been some random randy stranger pressed against her in a crowded train: that had been Josh's body signalling that it was ready, willing and able to mate with her...prepared to plant his seed deep inside her to start the next generation of Weatherbys.

And just thinking about the process of planting that seed was enough to have every hormone clamouring and her hands shaking enough to risk slopping the tea over the top of the mugs.

'Tea,' she announced brightly when she pushed open the door at his invitation. 'A dash of milk but no sugar,' she added, hoping that he wouldn't notice that there was a definite tremor to her voice. Well, it could hardly help shaking when her heart was beating hard enough to fill the room with rhythmic sound.

'To what do I owe this service?' he asked warily, and she nearly chuckled aloud.

'Oh, just look on it as a small thank you for a lovely meal last night,' she said with a happy smile, then deliberately slid her arm along his as she leant forward to deposit the tea in the space he'd hastily cleared for it.

She actually felt him flinch at the contact and for just a second found herself doubting her memories of the previous evening. Surely he didn't find her touch repellent? Then she heard him swallow hard and when she saw the way his nostrils flared slightly, as if he was deliberately breathing in the scent of her skin, she knew she hadn't been mistaken. He *was* aware of her as a woman, but was fighting it with everything he had.

'I'm off to tackle that daily mountain of paperwork, and chase up any outstanding lab results,' she said brightly as she made for the door with her own mug of tea, pausing just long enough to meet his eyes over her shoulder as she added, 'So you'll know where I am if you need me.'

She wasn't absolutely certain whether it had been humour or panic she'd seen in his eyes for that brief second before she pulled the door shut.

It was unlikely to be desire, she told herself sternly, no matter how much she wanted it to be. She really didn't have nearly enough experience of arousing a man to achieve it with a single one-liner and her first attempt at a sultry look.

'And I'm unlikely to find out, if he continues to be this elusive,' she grumbled towards the end of another long day.

Her head was aching from maintaining concentration for such a long time, and as for her legs and back…that many hours spent bending over tiny patients was going to give her a permanent stoop by the end of her six months on the unit.

And, quite apart from the number of children she treated along the way, it would be worth every bit of the discomfort if only it helped Josh to realise the possibility that there could be something more between them, she mused as she finally plodded her way up to her room, wincing at the sound of a furious argument raging in one of the nearby rooms.

Then she opened her own door and gasped at the sight that met her eyes.

There was water everywhere, and more flooding down through the ceiling as she watched.

'My books!' she shrieked and raced across to the desk to gather them up, more grateful than she could say that she'd stacked them into a neat pile before she'd left the room that morning.

She retreated to the doorway to examine them and breathed a sigh of relief.

The file on top was completely sodden, but apart from some damp corners, it looked as if the expensive texts had escaped relatively unscathed.

She couldn't say the same for her bed or her clothes.

'Dani! What's happened here? What have you done, girl?' demanded Marion as she joined her in the doorway, her Irish accent lilting in spite of her obvious shock at what she was seeing.

'It's not me. It's the idiot upstairs,' she snapped when she realised that there was no chance that she was going to get any study done that evening. It was going to take her for ever to get this mess sorted out—*if* she was going to get it sorted. How was she going to get her mattress dry enough to sleep on? 'Marion, could you do me a huge favour? Can you run up and hammer on the door to get them to turn the water off? Or get the caretaker with the master key to let you in to do it.'

Dani couldn't understand how this could have happened. Each of their rooms was equipped with a self-enclosed wet-room area that combined shower, toilet and hand-basin…one of the comedians in residence had said it made her think of the Orgasmatron in the Jane Fonda film *Barbarella*…but it should be impossible for water to leak, unless there'd been a catastrophic failure in the plumbing.

She stood there in the doorway, cuddling her precious books, while she listened to Marion running up the stairs and watched the water steadily saturate everything in sight.

'Magda!' she heard her friend shout to the accompaniment of a volley of thuds on the door. 'Magda Grayson! Open this door! There's water flooding through your floor!'

'I think I saw a stopcock in the laundry,' suggested one of the people who had begun to congregate in the corridor outside her door. 'I'll see if that stops it.'

Dani was now surrounded by exclamations of horror as her neighbours craned their necks to see the devastation growing by the minute in her room. She hated feeling helpless and it seemed to take for ever before someone answered the door upstairs, but finally she could tell that the water wasn't flowing quite so quickly any more.

'I found a stopcock. Did it do any good?' panted a voice from the back of the gathering throng.

'Something's made a difference,' Dani confirmed as the soggy sound of dripping finally began to slow, but whether it was the stopcock or the fact that someone had finally answered the door upstairs, she had no idea.

'Let me through, ladies and gentlemen,' Marion demanded as she bulldozed her way through the fascinated onlookers towards Dani's door. 'The water's been turned off, now, darlin', but I don't think it's going to do you much good tonight,' she commented. 'I think you'd better make some phone calls to find out if there's another room available.'

'How did this happen?' Dani demanded as she gazed at her soggy belongings in disbelief. 'Did one of the pipes spring a leak?'

'Not exactly,' Marion said, and raised her eyes pointedly to the room above before she finished quietly, 'Somebody…got distracted at the wrong moment and forgot that the shower was running.'

'What? How could anyone forget that they'd left it on? Surely it's automatic to turn it off when…' The expression on Marion's face was a picture and suddenly Dani realised exactly what had been going on in the room above hers to cause its occupants to forget they'd left the water running.

'The show's over, people,' Marion announced briskly, and Dani could easily imagine her in charge of a busy midwifery unit. 'Back to your own rooms—unless you're offering to help Dani mop up and sort through her soggy laundry.'

'Let me guess,' Dani growled when she handed her precious books over into Marion's hands for temporary safekeeping. 'Could it possibly be a certain male who thinks he's God's gift to women involved in this fiasco?'

'If you mean Tomasz, you're exactly right,' Marion said as she pushed her sleeves up and began to strip the bed. 'Apparently, a towel fell over the waste pipe but he and Magda were too…caught up in what they were doing to notice when the water started pouring out into the room, especially with his favourite "Music to Seduce by" DVD playing.'

Dani snorted, then caught Marion's eye over the gathering mountain of wet bedding and clothes. And suddenly the two of them were chuckling like idiots.

'I thought Magda was far too intelligent to be taken in by someone as obvious as Tomasz,' Dani said when she finally caught her breath, then wondered if she would have been equally as oblivious if she had been showering with Josh. As if she'd ever get the chance!

'There's no accounting for taste,' Marion said primly, and they were off again, but this time Dani knew there was a hint of envy in her own laughter.

'It's unlikely that the office will be open to find you another room at this time of night, so where are you going to stay?' Marion asked when the room had finally been dismantled, the mattress standing on its edge in the corridor, waiting to be carried down for disposal. A frown of concern pleated her wide freckled forehead. 'I'd offer to share with you but, small as you are, there'd never be room for you in a bed with someone of my *comfortable* proportions, and you'd never get any rest lying on the floor.'

'I'll make some phone calls,' Dani said vaguely, crossing her fingers that Josh would be back at his flat by now…and that he wouldn't be getting ready to go out on a hot date. Then she had to suppress the sudden surge of jealousy at the thought of Josh taking out some long-stemmed beauty.

'Josh?' she said tentatively when a husky male voice answered her call, the sound so sexy that she wondered whether he'd bothered taking his date out at all. Had they already made their way to the bedroom? Had she interrupted while they were…?

'Dani?' The voice sounded a little more like Josh, this time, but still…' What's the problem?' he asked with a degree of resignation that stung.

'I'm sorry to disturb you, but… What makes you automatically think that there's something wrong?' she demanded, piqued.

'Because you wouldn't have rung me otherwise—you'd have emailed,' he said gruffly, and he was quite right. She'd been so embarrassed by her birthday disaster that she'd all but cut off communication with him, even though she'd hungered for any scrap of contact. Only when he'd begun emailing her had she realised that it provided the degree of separation that she could cope with.

She would probably have chosen to email this time, if she'd been sure that she wouldn't electrocute herself in the disaster zone her room had become.

'Well, you're right,' she admitted grudgingly and found herself crossing her fingers that it wasn't his date's voice she could hear in the background.

'So, what's happened? Is it something on the unit? Everything was fine when I left, but I fell asleep in front of the news about a quarter of an hour ago.'

He'd been asleep? Was that why his voice had sounded so husky and sexy? Did he always sound that way when he was in bed, or…?

'No,' she said, quickly cutting off that train of thought before she forgot the reason for this call. 'As far as I know, everything on the unit's fine. It's a problem with my room,' she said with a grimace at the understatement.

'Another noisy party?' he asked. 'Are you angling for a free meal so you can get out of there until they turn the volume down?'

'Nothing as simple as that,' she owned up, even as she realised that she probably didn't even have a set of dry underwear to her name. 'My upstairs neighbour got a bit… absent-minded… And my room has been flooded.'

'Badly?' There was a sharper edge to his voice, telling her that his brain was once more firing on all cylinders. 'How much damage has it done to your things?'

'My books are mostly OK because I'd put a

folder on top of the pile and it acted as an umbrella, but pretty much everything else is soaked…my bed, my clothes… But I think my laptop has escaped.'

'You'll have to come over here, then,' he said decisively, and she breathed a sigh of relief that he'd offered. Somehow that felt much better than if she'd had to beg for a bed.

'I'll come straight over and collect you,' he continued, briskly. 'It shouldn't take me more than ten minutes to get there. Can you be ready by then?'

'No!' she exclaimed, horrified by the idea that everyone would know where she was going if Josh turned up outside her door to collect her. That sort of gossip was the last thing she needed if anyone on the unit was going to take her seriously. 'It'll take me at least half an hour to collect my things and organise laundry and notify the caretaker that he needs to arrange for disposal of the mattress. I'll get a taxi over as soon as I've finished, if that's all right?'

He was silent for so long that she began to wonder if the connection had been cut.

'Have you got your mobile phone with you? Is it still in working order?' he asked suddenly, taking her by surprise. Did he really think he'd need to check up on her to make sure she travelled safely? Did he think she was that incapable of looking after herself? 'I'll park in the public section of the car park—out of sight of any colleagues—and give you a ring to tell you where to find me. I take it that *was* why you didn't want me to come and collect you?'

Well, it *had* been, but she'd been thinking as much of his reputation as her own…not that he gave her the chance to explain that, because as soon as she agreed to his plan she was left with the sound of the dialling tone in her ear.

BB: The newlyweds send their love, said the message on her screen when Dani finally switched on her laptop, and she gave a huff of laughter.

She'd just gone through one of the most exhausting evenings of her life and there was that innocuous little line waiting for her.

Over the last few days, even while he'd seemed

to be keeping his distance from her, she'd often found a message waiting for her…a comment about something that had happened on the ward, perhaps, or a reminder of something she needed to do…almost as if he was deliberately reminding both of them of what he saw as his dual roles in her life, as professional mentor and big brother.

The irony this time was that Josh had been sitting in this very room when he'd typed it, probably at the very moment that she'd been discovering the water pouring through her ceiling. And now here she was ensconced in his study-cum-spare room with her pitiful belongings piled in the corner and the washing machine already churning through the first load of soggy clothing.

'Tea?' Josh called through the partially open door, and when she turned and saw him standing there with a brace of steaming mugs in one hand and a packet of chocolate biscuits in the other she nearly burst into tears.

This was just so very *Josh*.

He'd always been the very best big brother any girl could have had—endlessly supportive and patient and resigned from the day she'd taken her first wobbly steps to picking her up and dusting her off—but she'd been determined that this time she would show him that she was all grown up now, and didn't need rescuing any more.

She sighed silently and turned to clear a corner on the desk that held what was left of her most important belongings.

'How wet did your books get? Are they completely spoiled?' Josh demanded as he deposited his burden and reached for the top volume…an extremely expensive manual of paediatric X-ray diagnosis that had cost Dani an arm and a leg.

'They're not too bad, thank goodness—just a few damp corners—but the file of notes on top of them was completely ruined.' She pulled a face. 'That's going to take more than a few hours of solid slog to replace. They were the start of my revision notes for the next set of exams.'

His answering grimace told her he understood the significance of the loss. He would know that study time was hard to come by on a busy ward like theirs, and that by the time she was off duty, she was often too exhausted to concentrate properly.

'Didn't you keep a copy on your computer?' he asked, 'or were they all handwritten notes?'

'Some of each,' she admitted wearily as she sat in front of her laptop. 'I'd typed a lot of them up and printed them out, but I've no idea where or even if they are still on the computer as I only ever looked at the hard copy.'

'It's easy enough to find out.' He leaned forward over her shoulder to tap a couple of keys and brought up his own message onto the screen but Dani hardly noticed, every scrap of her awareness centred on the clean soapy smell of his skin just inches away from her.

'I didn't get your message until I switched on, just now,' she said hurriedly, gabbling the first thing that came into her head…anything to stop herself leaning towards him and breathing in the arousing combination of shampoo, laundry soap and potent male pheromones. 'Are they both well?'

'Mum is in seventh heaven cuddling all the grandchildren she's just acquired,' he said with a chuckle. 'With half of them she's not even sure there *is* a family connection, but she's not letting that worry her.'

'Well, she's been angling for you to produce some grandchildren for her to spoil for a long time,' Dani pointed out, aware, as ever, of the deep pang of jealousy that had clawed at her every time she'd thought of Josh having those grandchildren with one of the elegant women he'd dated from time to time. For so many years she'd ached with the need to carry those children for him, the perfect blend of his genes and hers joined together in one perfect baby.

'Yes!' he said, and for one crazy second she thought he was agreeing with her thoughts… until she saw the directory he'd pulled up on the screen. 'Looks like they are here. It's just the handwritten notes you *didn't* type in that you'll have to do again.'

'Thank you for that,' she said, disappointed when he immediately straightened away from her to retrieve his mug of tea, quite apart from her annoyance with herself at not knowing where she'd saved her notes. She hated seeming like the stereotypical dizzy blonde when she knew she had a good functioning brain under the hair…if only people would look beyond the unusual platinum blonde colour.

'Well, I'll leave you to get settled in,' Josh said briskly. 'Give me a shout if you need anything. The bathroom's through there…' He pointed to the door in the corner. 'The estate agent called it a Jack and Jill. Both bedrooms access the same bathroom from either side so you might need to check before entering, and there's a little cloakroom just inside the front door to save arguments.'

Dani was glad that he didn't look back over his shoulder at her as he left the room, certain that her eyes must almost be eclipsing her face in response to that news. It had been bad enough contemplating settling down in her borrowed bedroom, knowing that Josh was lying just yards away from her, but the thought that he would be just the other side of the wall while he stood naked under the shower… well, that was enough to send her pulse rocketing up into the stratosphere. And as for trying to sleep…that was probably going to be impossible.

CHAPTER SEVEN

SHE'D been right, she grumbled silently as she let herself out of Josh's flat the next morning.

Not long after she'd settled into bed, she'd heard Josh enter from his side of the bathroom and had pulled her pillow over her head to try to disguise the sound of the shower. But even though she'd managed to dull the sound, she hadn't been able to do anything about the flight of her imagination.

Not that she needed much imagination where Josh was concerned. Having lived in the same house as him for most of her life, it meant that she knew only too well exactly how broad his shoulders were and how long and strong his legs. What she hadn't anticipated had been the arousing detail that had appeared in her dreams, and the memories that had followed her into wakefulness were enough to make her blush.

'So where does all this leave me in my grand plan?' she mused under her breath as she strode briskly towards the hospital. 'Does the fact that we're now living together make things easier?' She paused for a huff of laughter at the thought of what the hospital grapevine would make of that little detail. Living together! She and the gorgeous, much sought-after consultant Josh Weatherby were actually living together. Please, God, no one would ever find out about it or the whole situation would become impossibly complicated.

Not that it wasn't complicated enough already.

She'd been determined that this six months' position would finally draw a line under her feelings towards him, one way or another. Either she would have to come to terms with the fact that her love for him was never going to be recipro-cated, or he would finally admit that she was the woman he'd been waiting for all these years.

'*As if,*' she mocked herself wryly. 'The fact that the thought of him having a shower can rob me of a night's sleep and make me blush is hardly likely to bowl him over with the realisation that I'm a mature woman, let alone that he's been waiting impatiently for me.'

But that didn't mean that she wasn't going to do her best to find out if there was any chance of her dreams coming true. As far as her career was concerned, she had an enormous amount to learn in the next few months and a decision to make about the future direction she was going to take in her career.

As far as her day-to-day relationship with Josh was concerned…well, she couldn't really make any decisions about that. She could hardly *force* the man to fall in love with her, neither could she seduce him into…

Her rambling thoughts came to a screeching halt with that single word.

Seduce?

Could she honestly see herself seducing Josh?

Her imagination told her she could, but as soon as she started trying to picture exactly how she'd go about it, she could feel the heat of a furious blush spread all the way from her throat to her hair.

You could, insisted an encouraging little voice inside her head, even as another, meaner one scoffed, *If you could ever get up the courage. Remember what happened the last time you tried?* that little voice continued. *You didn't even get past a kiss, so what hope have you got of achieving a full-scale seduction?*

Her shoulders slumped, knowing it was true. She'd read plenty of books and had her medical qualification, so she knew enough about the mechanics of sex to know what went where—'insert tab Y into slot X,' as one of her fellow students had described the process at its most basic level—but between her studies and the fact that she'd never been interested in any other man, she was woefully ignorant when it came to the practicalities and intricacies of what went on in the bedroom.

And, anyway, did she really want to force Josh into marrying her by seducing him? Was that really the way she would choose to start their life together, knowing that he would only have offered marriage because his over-developed sense of honour would insist on it?

No. What she wanted was for Josh to realise that, in spite of the fact he'd been taking care of her as the best of big brothers for the whole of her life, he loved her as the adult woman she'd become.

'And in the meantime…' she muttered under her breath with a groan at the end of far too many hours of worrying at the problem without coming to any reasonable conclusion.

In the meantime, life went on in its relentless way, with as many as one out of every eight newborn babies needing some sort of attention in their unit.

They were at full stretch at the moment, with every bed taken and every member of specialist staff rostered for every last second of their available hours.

'Sometimes I feel as if I'm trying to stop water coming out of a colander,' she complained to Marion as they bumped into each other in the lift going down to A and E. 'This is the fourth time this morning that they've asked for someone to come down, and with Josh away at some high-level meeting…'

'Oho! So it's Josh now, is it?' Marion teased, and Dani was grateful that they were the only ones in the lift, especially when she could feel the start of a blush sweeping up her throat and into her face.

'Of course we call him Josh,' she said, trying to achieve a lofty tone. 'We work with the man for a dozen hours a day, after all, and he's not the sort to stand on ceremony with his staff.'

'Well!' Marion exclaimed in disgust. 'I was really hoping that there was a bit of gossip to liven things up. I'm sick to death of the stories flying about the place about Tomasz's shenanigans. You wouldn't believe how huge the tales have grown in the telling!'

'Oh, yes, I would,' Dani countered. 'And it's a relief to speak to one of the few people who know, categorically, that there was *not* a red-hot orgy going on involving *all* the residents of the building.'

'Is that what they're saying now?' Marion asked with a burst of disbelieving laughter. 'Well, *I* certainly missed out if it was true, because I never saw a thing except for the water pouring from your ceiling.'

'You didn't miss anything much, if the other bit of gossip *is* true,' Dani consoled her with a grin of her own.

'Tell me. Tell me, quick!' Marion pleaded as the indicator told them they'd reached their destination.

'Nothing much,' Dani said dismissively as the doors started to slide open, just for the fun of teasing the woman, then relented to whisper, 'Just that the girls were passing around the information that a certain gentleman isn't quite as well endowed or as proficient in the use of certain equipment as he would have the world believe…'

'Ouch!' Marion said, and as she hurried to find the patient waiting for her, Dani could tell that her friend was kind-hearted enough to feel some sympathy for the younger man, if the ego-destroying tale was true, even as her eyes were glinting with the urge to laugh.

'Hello, it's me again!' she said when she reached her destination. 'Someone called up to unit for—'

'Follow me,' the staff nurse said without even

letting her finish speaking. 'Thank goodness you came so quickly. There's a preemie on the way that couldn't even wait to get upstairs, and the parents say it's at least eight weeks early.'

As a case history it was decidedly sketchy but, then, sometimes there just wasn't time for filling in forms, and this seemed to be one of them.

Dani paused a moment in the doorway to look at the situation, her own involvement obviously not necessary for a few more minutes. It wouldn't be long, though. The baby's head was already crowning.

She caught her first sight of the woman at the centre of the scurrying staff and for some reason her antennae twitched. The husband was clearly distraught, dividing his attention between his labouring wife and begging the midwife to save their baby.

The door behind her nudged one hip and Dani stepped aside to allow the warmed humidicrib to join the rest of the high-tech equipment in the room, but her eyes were somehow fixed on the dynamics of the couple. There was something about the way that the woman was clutching at the man's arm, as though she was trying to keep his focus on herself…an air of desperation, perhaps? Or was it fear? Or even guilt?

She shook her head to rid herself of such fanciful thoughts, forcing herself to concentrate, instead, on the head of the baby as it finally emerged into the world. It was a rather large head for a baby arriving a full two months early. Was that an indication that the baby was suffering from hydrocephalus? Would an operation be necessary to control the dangerous build-up of fluid within the skull?

She pulled a disposable apron over her head and swiftly tied it then snapped on a pair of gloves so that she would be ready to work quickly, if necessary, stepping closer so that she could see exactly what was happening.

Then the rest of the infant was delivered and for several seconds there was complete silence in the room, apart from the vigorous complaints from an obviously full-term baby.

'What's wrong?' the father demanded, his eyes

flicking frantically from Dani to the baby when she stepped up to the table to double-check the midwife's findings. 'Is there something wrong with the baby?'

'Absolutely nothing, as far as we can tell,' she reassured him, handing the baby into the new mother's arms, wondering how on earth they could have been told that a baby this size was two months premature. The greenest ultrasound technician would have known that the dates were wrong. 'This is a very healthy full-term baby, so there really isn't any need to worry. We just need to get him and his mum transferred to the maternity ward and—'

'That can't be right,' he interrupted with a frown, glancing from the midwife to Dani and back again. 'You said the baby's full term but it *can't* be. I wasn't even in the country nine months ago, so…' His eyes widened and his expression darkened as he stared down at his wife.

That was when Dani recognised the expression in the woman's eyes and realised that it was blatant fear.

'It's not my baby, is it,' he accused, and Dani noticed that the words hadn't sounded in the least like a question.

The new mother flinched and couldn't meet his gaze.

'Tell me!' he demanded, and Dani wondered if she was the only one who could hear the heart-break mixed in with his anger.

The baby was almost forgotten between them, the precious bundle clutched in his mother's arms while the tense drama played out over his newborn head.

A creak at the other side of the room drew Dani's attention to the doorway and the head that appeared around the edge. She had no idea of the man's name; all she knew from her frequent trips backwards and forwards from the unit was that he was one of the doctors in A and E.

Dark eyebrows lifted questioningly, silently asking whether his assistance was needed, and Dani gave a slight shake of her head, crossing her fingers that she was guessing right when he nodded and disappeared again.

'Tell me!' the distraught man repeated, snapping Dani's attention back to the tense situation as he reached out as though to grab his wife and force her to meet his gaze, force her to admit the awful truth.

Dani tensed, ready to step in to prevent any untoward happenings, but the baby clearly had other ideas.

Even as the angry man hesitated, obviously desperate for an answer but still civilised enough not to resort to physical violence to extract one, a little clenched fist escaped from the soft cloth wrapped around him.

Whether it was sheer accident or the result of fate, it collided with the powerful male hand hovering nearby and tiny starfish fingers instantly wrapped around the nearest finger and gripped tightly.

Someone drew in a sharp breath at the picture they made—the smallest, most helpless being in the room clinging to the biggest and strongest adult—but otherwise there was complete silence for several endless seconds.

'Martin, please,' the new mother whispered. 'Let me explain…when there aren't so many people around.'

'What's to explain?' he demanded, his eyes fixed on the trusting way that little hand was holding onto him, but it was obvious that most of the heat had gone out of his voice. All that was left was hurt and sorrow. 'He's someone else's baby, not mine.'

His regret was palpable as he gently slid his finger out of that tenacious grasp and stepped back out of reach.

'Martin…' she choked, reaching out towards him in panic as though she'd suddenly realised that he was deliberately creating distance between them.

'Who is it?' he demanded thickly, the words suddenly tumbling out of him in spite of his audience. 'Why did you marry *me* and let me think it was *my* baby you were carrying? Why didn't you call our wedding off and marry *him*?'

'I don't know,' she wailed suddenly, and everyone in the room was riveted, wondering how many more revelations they were going to be privy to. 'I don't *know* who…I was attacked…r-raped…and I didn't realise I was pregnant, not until after we were married, and I was just praying… hoping…that it *was* your baby and…and…'

She gasped as the contraction that heralded the final stage of her labour caught her by surprise, and the baby almost slid out of her grasp.

Dani reached out automatically to prevent the precious bundle from falling, but she was too slow. He was already firmly and safely grasped in big male hands.

'What's happening?' he demanded as his wife screwed up her face against the intensity of the pain, his continuing concern for her obvious in spite of the recent revelations. 'Has something gone wrong? Why is she in pain?'

'It's all right, Martin,' the midwife soothed as she checked progress. 'It's just the afterbirth coming away. Can you give me one last push, darling?' she added to the distraught young woman, and with those prosaic words, the atmosphere in the room almost returned to normal.

Not that any of them would be forgetting those tense few minutes in a hurry, Dani realised as she took the stairs back up to her own domain. It was almost a disappointment that she'd never hear the end of the story.

Except she felt she already knew how this particular tale was going to end, especially having seen the protective way that little boy had been cradled in a certain man's arms as he was led away to take part in the baby's first bath.

'No baby?' demanded a voice as soon as she stepped inside the unit. 'Didn't it make it? Too prem even for us?'

She turned to see Josh at the door of his office and her heart gave a convulsive leap in her chest when she saw the dark tawny hair curling at the V of his scrub top.

'Dani?' he prompted, and she hurriedly dragged her eyes away, then found that meeting his concerned golden gaze wasn't any easier on her pulse rate.

'Not prem enough,' she corrected. 'Mistaken dates, or something, because he's big and beautiful and healthy and doesn't need our help at all.'

'Good,' he said with a satisfied smile. 'That's the way we like them.' And he turned to go back into his office. 'Oh, before I forget.' He turned back, and as quick as she'd been to drag her eyes up from their appreciation of his sexy rear view, she knew the sudden heat in her cheeks was a giveaway—the narrow-eyed glitter lancing in her direction told her so. 'We've had a call from Barchester. They need to transfer one across to us. They've run out of beds.'

'Again!' she exclaimed, trying to remember how many times it had been since she'd joined the department that they'd been contacted to accept a sick baby transferred halfway across the country. It was such a dangerous thing to do when they were so fragile.

'It's not as if we've got any spare capacity,' she pointed out. 'If that baby down in A and E hadn't been healthy…'

'I know. I'd have been frantically trying to decide which of the babies was strong enough to be moved out of the unit and into a specialled bed on Paediatrics,' he said on a heavy sigh, raking his hand through his hair and clenching it in a gesture of frustration. 'It's the same story over and over again. We're desperately short of qualified staff because the hospital won't pay them enough, so we can't cope with any more patients on the unit. And at the same time, the administrators are wasting precious money giving the conference rooms and top-echelon offices fancy makeovers.'

'Well, we wouldn't want them to be uncomfortable while they sit in their comfy chairs counting all the beans and shuffling them from one pile to another,' Dani chided with heavy sarcasm.

A wry smile lifted one corner of his mouth. 'I know. I know. I'm preaching to the choir,' he admitted. 'But if you knew how fatuous so many of the meetings I have to go to are, and how much precious time they waste while they stuff platefuls of chocolate biscuits down their greedy throats…'

'Chocolate biscuits!' Dani exclaimed. 'You've been going to meetings and been supplied with chocolate biscuits and you haven't brought any back for me!'

'Get onto Barchester for an update on that transfer,' he ordered sternly, and she threw him a cheeky salute as she left the room. She was smiling broadly as she waited for the call to be answered, her spirits bubbling at the memory of his expression. He'd never been able to hide the gleam of laughter in his eyes when it came to her passion for chocolate.

'This is Ricky Tomlins…the transfer you've been expecting from Barchester,' said a tall blonde with a folder tucked under her arm.

'That's right,' Dani said with a smile, and held her hand out for the patient's notes, keen for the handover to take place as smoothly as possible. The sooner the little boy was settled into the controlled surroundings of the unit the better. By all accounts, he'd already got enough of a struggle on his hands without being dragged all over the country.

'Oh. Isn't Mr Weatherby ready?' the woman

said, tightening her grip on the folder. 'Shouldn't you be letting him know we're here?'

'Mr Weatherby has been informed,' Dani said. 'I'm Dr Dixon and I'll be documenting this little chap's arrival. If you'd like to follow me, we can deal with the paperwork while Nadia supervises his transfer into the unit.'

The woman was clearly unwilling to accept those arrangements and Dani didn't know whether to stifle a groan at the fact that she'd obviously been looking forward to seeing Josh rather than his female underling, or to admit that she was jealous of yet another tall, slender, beautiful woman in his life.

Well, he obviously wasn't that eager to see her or he'd have been here to meet her, the sensible voice inside her head pointed out, and she found a measure of pity for the woman's obvious disappointment. *And if she knew that you are sharing his flat*, the wicked voice added, and she felt a smug grin inch its way upward.

Not that sharing his flat had done her any good,

so far, she admitted wryly as she checked the documentation of little Ricky's progress since his precipitate arrival in the world. In fact, the only progress *she'd* made had been to develop some very unattractive shadows under her eyes as she tried to ignore the fact that his bed was just the other side of the bathroom from hers. Added to that was her wake-up call every morning as she lay there and listened to the splash of water while he took his shower, trying not to picture his naked body just inches away from her.

'Tell Mr Weatherby that Jillian Treacher sends her best wishes,' the elegant woman said as the team gathered up their portable equipment and prepared to make the return journey to Barchester. There was a note of pleading in her voice and for just a moment Dani almost felt sorry enough for her to pass the message on.

'Of course,' she said, meeting the perfectly made-up eyes, but with a flash of that instant communication that the female half of the world understood when a desirable man was involved, they both knew that she wouldn't.

'How's he doing?' she asked Nadia as soon as she'd scrubbed and donned gloves and apron.

'His pulse and respiration are a little higher than they should be,' the specialist nurse pointed out with a glance at the bank of monitors.

'It could just be caused by the stress of being moved about,' Dani suggested as she compared the readings with those in the file. 'Keep an eye on him and give me a shout if you're still not happy. I'm just going to let Josh know he's settled in, in case he wants to come and give the little chap a once-over.'

Dani was pleased that Josh had the confidence in her to leave her to handle the new arrival, but she would still be glad of his input, especially with the levels of some of the drugs little Ricky was receiving.

'Have you got a minute?' she asked when his voice bade her enter his office and he looked up from the never-ending mountain of paperwork.

'That depends,' he countered with a wary glance past her shoulder towards the hallway. 'Has she gone?'

Dani chuckled at his expression and her jealousy vanished as if it had never existed. 'If you mean the lovely Jillian Treacher, yes, she's gone…but she left a message to pass on her best wishes to you,' she added, suddenly inexplicably confident that the woman's relationship with Josh was no threat.

Not that *she* had anything to boast about in the relationship stakes. For all the notice Josh had paid to her since she'd moved into his flat, she might as well have been a piece of the furniture. If she'd been expecting him to suddenly realise that he was in love with her and declare that he wanted her around for ever, she would have been very disappointed.

'Was that all you wanted—to pass on the message?' he asked with a hint of impatience.

'No. It was about the new transfer.' She stepped forward to place the file on his desk. 'He's called Ricky Tomlins and he was ten weeks prem. You can see from the size of the file that he's had a rocky start, but…I'm a bit concerned about some of the dosages he's on, and the fact that his pulse and respiration are raised in spite of them. Would you like to—?'

'Tell me what you think is wrong and what you want to do about it,' he interrupted, leaning back in his chair without opening the file, those dark golden eyes fixed on her as though he wanted to be able to read her mind.

For a moment Dani was nonplussed when he didn't immediately reach for the file, wondering what he was doing. It was only when he did that annoying trick of raising one eyebrow at her that she realised he was giving her the chance to show how much she'd learned so far; that he wanted her to have the courage of her own convictions and the confidence to stand by her deliberations.

After that, it was easy to explain her concern that the other hospital might have left the little boy on too high a dose of several drugs purely for convenience, knowing that they were going to have to ship him out to another unit, and that this might be having an adverse effect on his own body's slowly developing control systems.

'So, what are you proposing? Stopping those

drugs?' His voice was deceptively mild but she could hear the underlying challenge to justify what she'd decided was the right course of action.

'Stopping some...yes, replacing others... probably, but doing nothing immediately so that he has time to relax and settle down after the journey,' she said firmly. 'His parents have only just caught up with him and they need a little time to get to know us and our regime before they'll start to trust us.'

Josh was smiling by the time she stopped to draw breath.

'It sounds as if you've got everything under control,' he said, and she glowed inside. 'I'll go through the file in the next half an hour, then come out to meet Ricky and his parents.' He tapped a thoughtful finger on the manila cover of the file. 'Any other problems? Anything else you want?'

Apart from you? the voice in her head said, but she shook her head. 'Nothing at the moment. Megan's actually put on a little weight, but she's still forgetting to breathe sometimes. Her mum's getting really good at flicking the bottom of her foot to get her started again. Apart from that, there are several sets of test results due back from the labs soon. I'll get them entered in the relevant files as soon as they arrive.'

'Good. Nag them a bit, to make sure they haven't just forgotten to send them through. I'll go over them after I've spoken to Ricky's parents, then we can—'

The strident ring of the phone interrupted him and the quick frown that followed whatever the caller was saying didn't bode well.

'She needs to come in as soon as possible,' he said shortly. 'Bring her directly to the unit without wasting time in A and E. We'll be waiting for her.' He was already on his feet by the time the call ended.

'What's the matter?' Dani's pulse was already racing with the prospect of an emergency admission. That was certainly what it had sounded like.

'A home birth has hit some problems. The little girl became distressed during the delivery, but the mother was determined to have her perfect natural delivery and refused to be transferred.' His anger at the selfishness of the unknown woman couldn't have been more obvious. 'The baby's inhaled meconium…rather a lot of it, apparently.'

Dani swore under her breath as she followed his long-legged strides out of the room, this time needing to jog to keep up with him. Having a baby inhale the black sticky substance that had formed in the foetal bowel could be bad news…very bad news, with complications ranging from impaired breathing to brain damage or even death. Apart from the fact that the delivery hadn't immediately been transferred to the hospital when things had started to go amiss, what on earth had gone wrong that the midwife hadn't suctioned the foul stuff away before the newborn had taken her first breath?

'Where on earth are we going to put her?' she demanded while she still had breath of her own. 'Now that Ricky's arrived from Barchester, we haven't got a cot free to put her in, or the staff to special her. I know if everything goes well that her treatment should be mainly supportive after the first few hours, but initially her care is going to be very time-consuming.'

'We're going to have to play roulette with babies' lives… again!' he said grimly as he began a lightning circuit of the isolettes to try to decide which of the babies might be strong enough to leave them.

When the paramedic carried the newborn into the unit, closely followed by a colleague laden with oxygen and primary portable monitoring equipment, Dani's heart sank. She could actually hear the little grunt that came with every breath right across the room, in spite of the muffling effect of the oxygen mask.

'Bring her in here.' She beckoned, indicating the theatre anteroom. 'We're still trying to make space for her and it'll take a few more minutes before everything's been set up.' Apart from anything else, the bay where she would soon be installed was having the usual stringent clean before she was admitted to make sure there was no chance of adding a hospital-acquired infection to her woes.

Not that little Sima, the previous occupant, had suffered any ill-effects from her stay there. The tiny girl's recovery from major cardiac surgery had been almost miraculous, but neither Josh nor Dani were happy with shipping her out of their care quite so quickly.

'She hasn't had any pulmonary lavage,' the paramedic warned as he deposited his tiny charge on the trolley, automatically positioning her so that the foul meconium wouldn't be sliding any deeper into the lungs. 'In spite of the oxygen, she's breathing too fast and she's already starting to become cyanosed.'

'What about her pulse?' Dani reached out with gentle fingers, hoping to find a reassuring steady beat.

'Tachycardic,' the man said succinctly, confirming what her fingers were telling her and dashing her hopes.

'How is she doing?' There was concern in Josh's voice but it was the warm husky burr so close behind her that had Dani's nerves tingling. 'We're ready to settle her into her new bed if

she's… Damn!' he exclaimed when the little
body suddenly stiffened under their eyes and
began to convulse.

CHAPTER EIGHT

'WHAT have you done to my baby?' wailed a voice at the doorway, and Dani spared a swift glance for the figure in the wheelchair, guessing that this was the unfortunate child's mother.

'She breathed some muck in during the delivery and it's interfering with her breathing,' Josh explained tersely, even as he was drawing up an anticonvulsant into a small syringe.

'What are you giving her?' the woman demanded. 'I don't want her to be filled with un-necessary drugs.'

They all paused for a fraction of a second and Dani could almost hear Josh's brain considering exactly how to reply…politely.

'Do you want me to throw the drugs away and let your daughter die in the next couple of minutes, or shall I administer this and give her a chance to live?' he challenged frankly, the needle gleaming sharply under the unforgiving lights as he held it out towards her in his gloved hand.

All the staff knew that if the parents refused to allow the vital treatment, the hospital could have the baby made a ward of court so that they could do whatever was necessary to try to save her life, but that would take time that this sick infant just didn't have, not if they were to minimise her chances of suffering permanent brain damage from lack of oxygen.

'D-die?' the woman stammered, her face visibly draining of colour. 'B-but…she only got some muck in her face as she was being born. They all come out looking a bit mucky…don't they?' She glanced wildly from one face to another and they could almost see her willing them to agree with her.

'This was more than a bit mucky,' Dani said, stepping towards the confused young woman. 'The stuff your baby breathed in is a cross between…between superglue and toxic waste, and at the moment it's damaging your daughter's breathing so badly that the rest of her body just can't cope on its own. She just needs help. That's all we want to do, I promise you…help her while she's struggling so badly.'

The new mother's eyes were bloodshot and full of panic but her gaze clung to Dani's as though she were a life raft in a perilous sea.

'Please,' she whispered through bloodless lips. 'Save my baby. Save my Rosie.'

Dani felt a brief spark of satisfaction that she'd gained permission but when she turned back to the shuddering little figure on the trolley she realised that Josh had already administered the antispasmodic while the decision was being made.

'Jumped the gun a bit, didn't you?' she muttered under her breath as she rejoined him, knowing just what a risk he'd taken with his professional standing. The hospital's legal department would have been the ones going into seizures if they'd known.

'I never had a moment's doubt that you'd be able to persuade her,' he murmured back even as he swiftly drew a blood sample. 'I've been on the losing end of the pleading expression in those blue eyes for too many years.'

The eyes in question took a quick panicked look around, trying to see whether any of the other staff had noticed his unwary reference to the fact that they'd known each other for a long time. Until that moment he'd been so careful, for both their sakes, not to let that little item get out.

Anyway, it wasn't true. She hadn't spent all those years trying to persuade him to do things for her…had she?

'I can hear your brain whirring,' Josh said, and she realised to her horror that she had absolutely no idea just how long she might have been standing there mulling over his words. 'Are you happy to transfer Rosie?'

'Rosie?' She blinked, wondering how much she'd missed. Who on earth was Rosie?

Josh's pointed glance down at the strangely still figure in front of them brought her back up to speed. 'Her bed was almost ready when we came in here,' he continued. 'But now that we've stopped the seizure, we really need to get her into Theatre and see if we can clean her up a bit.'

'Theatre?' The new mother's fears came spilling over again in spite of the fact that her husband was now standing behind her with his hands cradling her shoulders and stroking them soothingly. 'You're not going to operate on her!'

'Of course not,' Josh agreed easily. 'It's just that we'll have a bit more room in there than we've got in here, and the lighting's a bit better to see if we can wash the muck out of her.'

Without another word needing to be spoken, their newest patient was transferred through the batwing doors, leaving her parents firmly on the other side.

'Connect her up to all the monitors,' Josh said briskly. 'Who's the anaesthetist on duty? Is he on his way? I want constant readings on her blood gases while we do pulmonary lavage. We'll need to suction mouth, pharynx and trachea and bag-ventilate between lavages with high concentrations of oxygen.'

As the scene played out around her, Dani began to wonder if she'd ever be good enough to take on a job like this. Josh made it seem almost effortless, barely pausing for breath before he was issuing his next request or performing the next procedure.

She felt quite wrung out when it was finally time to transfer Rosie to the warmth of the waiting humidicrib, and Josh was still issuing directions.

'Monitor temperature and humidity,' he said briskly to one of the more senior nurses, and Dani wondered exactly when he'd managed to organise for her to special their newest charge— he'd been fully occupied from the second that Rosie had arrived.

'And measure every millilitre of fluid in and out to give us warning of any kidney problems,' he continued, almost without drawing breath. 'Her chest is noisy—as it would be after everything that's happened in the last hour—but keep an ear open for any changes, in case she's starting to develop an infection from the gram-negative bacteria. God forbid she gets chemical pneumonia,' he added fervently, and Dani silently echoed the thought.

It would be tempting to add prophylactic anti-biotics to the mixture of treatments she was receiving, especially for gram-negative bacteria, but she knew that it was better to hold off, keeping the drugs in reserve in case she actually showed signs of infection. Her little body had enough to cope with at the moment.

Dani was casting one last glance over her shoulder as she left the room when a lean arm suddenly wrapped around her shoulder and gave her an unexpected hug.

'You did well,' Josh said with a smile that instantly doubled her heart rate. Every inch of her body registered the impulsive contact, relishing the sensation from her shoulders right down to her knees.

He was so hard and strong against her, the person she'd depended on and leant on for so much of her life. And he was so warm, and she could even hear the steady thump of his heart under her ear where it pressed against the muscular wall of his chest.

Her knees started to buckle and she drew in a

swift breath to try to regain control, but that only drew in the familiar mixture of the same shampoo and soap that had lingered in the shower this morning, this time combined with overtones of healthy virile male.

Her pulse started to race at the intimate images that started to form inside her head and she only had a few seconds to register the fact that Josh's heartbeat had grown noticeably faster, too, before his arm was abruptly withdrawn and he was standing with the full width of the corridor between them.

Her brain scrambled to understand exactly what had just happened, but all she could come up with was the echo of his words of praise.

'I didn't really do anything,' she said, silently cursing the unexpectedly husky edge to her voice. 'You were doing all the important things.'

'And you somehow managed to anticipate me at every stage so that I barely had to ask for a thing,' he pointed out seriously. 'Given that you've been in the unit such a short time, I was really impressed that your instincts were so good.'

Was it her instincts?

Dani wasn't so sure as she replayed that fraught time in her head. Yes, she'd been able to find the right words to persuade Rosie's mother to trust them to do what was right for her precious daughter, but how much of the rest had been the fact that she felt a special kind of connection with Josh?

She stifled a laugh, glad that no one could hear what she was thinking or she'd end up being sent for psychiatric evaluation.

But it was true, nevertheless. For a long time she'd had the feeling that there was a unique empathy between the two of them that enabled her to know what he was thinking and feeling and...

'What rubbish!' she scoffed aloud, then remembered where she was and continued in a mutter under her breath. 'If you really knew what he was thinking and feeling, you would know exactly how he feels about you...and you don't!'

Oh, she knew that he had always cared about her from the moment she'd been born, as a big brother cared about his little sister, but that wasn't what she wanted now.

'And I honestly haven't got a clue how he feels about that,' she grumbled crossly, and only then realised that perhaps she *had* warranted the praise that Josh had dealt out this morning. If it hadn't been some non-existent mystical connection between them that had helped her to anticipate his needs, perhaps it *had* been the fact that her medical and clinical instincts were growing.

But she really didn't have time to think about herself, not with the unit bursting at the seams and so many of their patients critically ill.

It seemed as if she and Josh were kept running from one baby to the other with crisis after crisis, sometimes almost colliding as they hurried to respond to the shrilling monitors.

It was gone two in the afternoon before Dani decided she simply had to take a break, not just because her body was desperate for a serious intake of calories but because she hadn't been near a bathroom for more hours than was sensible.

'That feels better,' she murmured as she washed her hands, then jumped when someone behind her laughed.

'I know what you mean,' Nadia said ruefully. 'The rules might say that we're entitled to so many minutes break per shift, or whatever, but they must have been dreamed up by someone who's never actually worked in a hospital.'

'As if patients are just going to miraculously not need us because some bean-counter decrees it's time for a little…relief,' Dani agreed with feeling. 'It would be different if there were enough members of staff to cover for us while we had a drink or something to eat, but that would mean paying an extra salary or two, and they wouldn't do that, not when we're mugs enough to cover for each other.'

'Still, I wouldn't swap my job for something at a desk,' Nadia said as they made their way back out into the corridor. 'The pay and conditions are terrible and there's so much heartbreak along the way when some of the tinies don't make it, but when one of them does…'

'It makes everything worthwhile,' Dani finished for her, in total agreement.

'Especially when you've got a boss like ours,' Sally joined in with a sly nod towards Josh's familiar figure. 'What that man does for a pair of crumpled scrubs!'

Dani felt the familiar heat start to creep up her throat and silently cursed her pale complexion, then decided there was only one way to deal with the situation—to play up to it.

'Tell me about it!' she joked, flapping a hand in front of her face as if to fan the heat away. 'A butt that perfect ought to be made illegal, especially in thin cotton pyjamas.'

Nadia chuckled, then had to swiftly stifle her laughter when Josh turned to look at the two of them through the glass wall. 'Do you think he heard us?' she hissed with sparkling dark eyes.

Dani shook her head, but she knew from the expression she'd caught in his eyes that he *had* heard her remark. The thing she hadn't been able to tell was what he'd thought about it.

* * *

BB: We need to make a grocery run.

Josh paused with his fingers resting on the computer keys and groaned aloud at the prosaic message. It wasn't what he'd wanted to say, not after the conversation he'd overheard earlier today.

If any of the babies had been crying, he probably wouldn't have heard a thing, but they'd all been blessedly quiet for a few moments and the words had reached him all too clearly.

'*A butt that perfect ought to be made illegal,*' Dani had said, and when their eyes had met, she'd known he'd heard her, but what he didn't know was whether she'd only said it in fun or whether she really thought he had a perfect butt.

'For heaven's sake! How juvenile can you get!' he admonished himself, appalled at how pleased he'd been at the thought she'd been looking at his body and liked what she saw.

Those were dangerous thoughts, especially now that she was living with him.

'Correction,' he growled when his body responded all too predictably to that thought. 'Now that she's sharing the flat.'

And then there was the message he'd just sent her. As soon as he'd pressed the button he'd realised just how cosily familiar it sounded, as if they were an old married couple leaving the modern equivalent of the note on the kitchen table.

The crazy thing was, even though he knew it was an impossibility, he'd like nothing better than to know that they would be coming home to the same place every night for the rest of their lives.

It was driving him round the bend at the moment, to walk in the front door and just know from the way the air felt that she hadn't arrived home yet. And as for following her through the bathroom, when the whole room was filled with the lingering scent of her soap and one end of the shelf had a collection of her jars and bottles all set out in a neat little row, the way she always arranged them...

He'd even found himself reaching for one of them this morning, tempted to open it and breathe in the familiar scent so that he could pretend that she was standing nearby.

'Pathetic!' he accused himself with a stern shake of his head. 'The sooner she finds somewhere else to live, the better.' But even as he said the words he knew he was lying. He knew it was a temporary situation and that she would eventually move out...would eventually meet a man and marry him and *he* probably wouldn't see her more than a couple of times a year...

His heart clenched inside his chest at the thought, already prepared to hate the man who took her away from him permanently. It would happen, sooner or later, he had no doubt about that. How could he have, knowing Dani the way he did, and knowing the way other men responded to her? The only surprise was that she seemed so totally unaware of the way her petite perfection affected the rest of his gender.

'I give up,' he growled and flung his hands up, knowing that he had little chance of thinking about anything else while he sat there. He might just as well go out and do the shopping as wait for her to arrive. He might have a better chance of concentrating on something else if he was jostling his way through a crowded supermarket.

He was just thrusting his arms into his jacket sleeves when he heard the sound of Dani's key in the door.

'Going somewhere?' she asked brightly, but he could almost fool himself into believing that there was a hint of disappointment in her expression. Had she actually been looking forward to seeing him again?

'Shopping,' he said shortly, telling himself he was a fool for indulging in wishful thinking. 'The fridge is empty. Any preferences?'

'You mean, apart from anything containing chocolate?' she said with that irresistibly impish grin.

'I mean, real food.' He tried to be stern, but he already knew that it was a lost cause. No one could lighten his mood the way Dani could. There was just something so bright and shining about her attitude to life that it seemed to spread to everyone around her.

'You mean, chocolate's not one of the major

food groups? It would be possible to live *without* eating it.' She deposited the bag containing her study books on the end of the kitchen counter, grabbed a couple of shopping bags and her purse and was standing in front of the door in a matter of seconds. 'Ready to go?' she asked, as eager as a puppy waiting to go for a walk.

Not for the first time Josh was impressed by the fact that Dani was so supremely unconcerned by her appearance that she hadn't even thought to say she needed some time to change her clothes and apply make-up.

'Ready,' he agreed and reached for the catch, only realising when his fingers wrapped around hers that she'd reached it first.

Her fingers were as slender and dainty as a child's, and the skin was so much softer and paler than his own that he didn't seem to be able to drag his eyes away from the contrast.

'Josh?' There was a definite quiver in her voice and he suddenly realised that he must have been standing there staring down at their entwined fingers for some time.

'Sorry,' he said, dragging his hand away in a hurry so that she was finally free to open the door. 'Got distracted… thinking about what we need to buy.'

And if she believed that, just a few miles away there was a beautiful old stone-built bridge he could sell her…

The shops weren't far enough away to make it worthwhile taking the car, not with the amount of traffic on the roads, and much to his relief the number of pedestrians made it difficult to walk together long enough to carry on a conversation.

Once they were in the shop it was a different matter and he suddenly realised that this was the first time that the two of them had gone shopping together since she'd been a schoolgirl.

'Any dietary preferences?' he asked as they set off down the aisle stacked with more varieties of fruit and vegetables than he could name.

'Not me!' she said with an infectious giggle. 'Don't you remember? I'll eat anything that stands still long enough for me to get my teeth into it.'

'Don't remind me,' he groaned, suddenly remembering that she seemed to have been born with her metabolism permanently stuck on high speed. From the moment that tiny little scrap of humanity had decided that she was going to fight for life, she'd taken to food with a single-minded intensity that had only been replaced by her studies once she'd decided she wanted to follow him into medicine. 'You could always eat like a pig without ever putting on an extra ounce. It used to drive Mum to distraction, especially when people asked if she was feeding you properly.'

Her laughter pealed out, drawing smiling glances all around, and suddenly it seemed as though the whole tiresome task of shopping had become pleasurable entertainment, over far too soon.

'Shall we grab a bite to eat on the way home?' he heard himself suggesting and wondered what had happened to his common sense. It hadn't been too difficult to persuade himself that this was nothing more than the sort of shopping trip that they'd undertaken for so many years during her childhood, but it was something else again to deliberately spend time together in more secluded surroundings.

'We can't,' Dani said, almost as if she'd heard his inner debate, then added prosaically, 'We've got to take the frozen stuff home before it defrosts. Anyway, there isn't much point in buying all this stuff if you're intending eating out. *And* it costs more.' She feigned a glare in his direction. 'We aren't all on a consultant's salary, you know. Some of us have to watch our pennies.'

And that was just another reason why he couldn't step over the line.

He had already attained his consultancy while she was just starting out on her career. And she was such a fiercely independent girl...*woman*, he corrected himself quickly...that she would hate it if any colleagues were to think that her achievements had been as a result of a relation-ship with him.

'But that means cooking,' he pointed out, then added with a grimace, 'And washing up.'

'You've got a dishwasher, for heaven's sake!' she exclaimed as she efficiently emptied the items out of the trolley then packed them into bags once they'd been scanned.

When he didn't comment she fixed him with keen blue eyes then grinned widely.

'Don't tell me!' she crowed. 'You've never used it!'

'Only because I'm never home enough to use enough dishes to fill it,' he said defensively as he got out his wallet.

'That's crazy!' She glared at him, her pride obviously piqued when he refused her silent offer of cash towards her half of the bill, but she didn't miss a beat in their conversation. 'You've been cooking ever since I can remember. You used to do it every night that Mum was on duty…and breakfast in the mornings when she was on earlies.'

'Yes, well, it always seemed more worthwhile when there were two to cook for. It hardly seems worth all the effort just for one, especially when I get stuck with the clean-up duty as well.'

'Well, there are two of us now,' she pointed out firmly, and he was glad that she didn't know anything about the flood of awareness that little phrase caused inside him. 'We can go back to the old routine—whichever one does the cooking, the other one has to clear away afterwards. OK?'

He agreed for the sake of peace, knowing that she would argue her point for ever once she'd decided her idea was the most logical, but the whole situation caused a strange hollow feeling inside him.

On the surface, it was so close to everything he'd ever dreamed of—having Dani as a permanent part of his life—and yet in reality it couldn't have been further away from it. Yes, she was living in his house and they would be sharing cooking and cleaning duties, but what he really wanted…well, that would be for ever impossible and it was time he stopped thinking about it.

In the end, he had cooked while Dani had sorted the last of her laundry and ironed them each a shirt for the following morning.

It was such an ordinary task, one that was probably being performed in thousands of homes right across the country at exactly the same time, but there was something about the sight of those slender fingers stroking and patting the fine white cotton into position that had drawn his attention as surely as if he'd been wearing the shirt and she'd been smoothing it along his arms, across his chest and down his body.

In spite of his best efforts, that image had lingered hotly in his head so that by the time he'd finished eating he'd been so uncomfortable that all he'd been able to think of doing was taking a very long, very cold shower.

Unfortunately, that had little effect, especially when he went to bed almost blue with the cold and had to listen to Dani showering just inches away from his bed.

'Rosie's temperature's up' were the first words Dani heard when she entered the unit the next morning and she was hard put not to groan aloud.

She'd thought it was hard concentrating after a sleepless night due to the constant noise around her room in the staff accommodation, but she was no better off at Josh's flat. Not because it was noisy. It wasn't. Its position near the top of the purpose-built block and the high-spec sound insulation that had obviously been incorporated at the building stage meant that only the sound of emergency sirens reached her room, and even that was muffled by the double glazing.

No, it was purely because she was so aware that Josh was there in the flat, just feet away, and she'd be lying in her own bed, imagining him in that spacious double bed with plenty of room for her to join him and…

Was she ever going to feel as if she was alert enough to give her usual one hundred and one per cent effort to her profession again?

'What about her kidney function? Is she still producing urine?' Dani held her hand out for the latest input-output figures. She blinked when she saw Josh's signature on the antibiotic dosage prescribed in the early hours of the morning. It looked as if he'd had even less sleep than she had, but at least he'd had the excuse of a looming crisis with one of their little charges.

'It was dropping off badly until the drugs got

into her system. So far, it hasn't got any worse, but we'll have to wait for the antibiotics to get properly into her system to see whether they knock the infection on the head.'

And that would take more than a few minutes to happen, Dani knew from past bitter experience as she watched the little body struggling for each breath in spite of the ventilator. Little Rosie had so few reserves to draw on to fight such a catastrophic battle so soon after birth. There was a serious possibility that she might not recover from one bad decision made at the wrong moment, in spite of the round-the-clock care she was now receiving.

An anguished hiccup behind her told Dani that Rosie's mother had returned to her baby's side, her tear-reddened eyes telling their own story of how the poor woman had obviously spent the night.

'Have you ever wished you could turn back the clock, even for a few minutes?' she asked Dani as she lowered herself gingerly into the chair beside the clear plastic cot. 'I was just so certain that having her in my own home was the best thing for her…the most natural way of giving birth, so that I could feel comfortable and in control, so that there was no chance that I'd be brow beaten into accepting drugs I didn't want.'

Dani murmured wordlessly, just enough to let her know she was listening and to encourage her to let her tormenting thoughts out.

'When the midwife said she wanted me to transfer to hospital for the delivery, I shouted at her…accused her of cheating me into thinking I was going to have a home birth when she'd always intended forcing me to come in… And I refused to listen when she tried to explain…refused to accept that anything could possibly go wrong when I'd planned everything down to the last detail.'

The tears were pouring down her face as she was recounting her tale and Dani would have comforted her but for the fact that she had a feeling that the woman needed to talk about the situation more than she needed to be hugged.

'It's all my fault,' she continued, hollow-eyed as she gazed in despair at her precious daughter. 'My baby's dying and it's all my fault.'

That was something that Dani could argue, and did, immediately.

'Your baby's *not* dying,' she said firmly, 'not if any of us in the unit have anything to say about it.' This time she didn't hold back but wrapped a comforting arm around the trembling shoulders.

'She's going to be all right?' Hope was stark on her face. 'You promise me that she's going to be all right?'

'I can't promise that,' Dani said honestly, much as she would have liked to. 'Not yet… But we're giving her antibiotics for the infections she's developed as a result of breathing in the meconium, and it already looks as if they're starting to have an effect.'

'Can't you do anything to hurry them up? Give her a stronger dose, or something?'

'If only it were that easy,' Dani said wryly. 'Unfortunately, it's just a matter of waiting and praying and letting her know that the most important person in her world is right here beside her.'

That made her blink. 'You think she knows I'm here?' Disbelief was warring with hope.

'I'm sure of it,' Dani said. 'So it's very important that you talk to her in the same voice you
used while you were waiting for her to arrive, so
she recognises you. And that means no more
tears…unless you cried all the way through your
pregnancy?'

'No,' the poor woman choked, almost surprised into a chuckle at the thought. 'Actually, I
sang to the baby…a lot.'

'Anything in particular?' Dani was intrigued.
'Nursery rhymes? Pop music?'

'Opera,' she admitted diffidently, and it was
Dani's turn to blink. 'I started by singing along
with the radio, years ago, and ended up taking
lessons and joined a choir, but I couldn't possibly
do that in here.'

'Why not?' Dani challenged. 'As long as you
don't go into full Wagnerian mode in the middle
of the night, I don't suppose anyone will mind.
I can always ask Mr Weatherby if he has any objections, but I don't expect he will, especially if
it helps Rosie.'

She didn't need the way the woman's eyes travelled to something behind her shoulder to know that Josh had just come into the room and was now standing behind her. It seemed as if she was aware of his proximity with every pore of her skin.

'Mr Weatherby has no objections as long as it doesn't upset anyone else,' he said with a twinkle in those warm golden eyes. 'Just keep it soft and gentle and we'll probably all enjoy it. You've probably noticed that special care baby units aren't the most relaxed places on the planet.'

His matter-of-fact acceptance of the idea went a long way towards making Rosie's mother feel a little less helpless and hopeless, but it also confirmed Dani's feelings of admiration for the man.

She sighed as she watched him walk away after he'd checked over Rosie's latest figures, unable to prevent her eyes following all the way across the room until she heard Nadia's soft chuckle beside her.

'What that man does for a pair of baggy pyjamas…not that you've noticed,' teased her colleague, and Dani's face instantly flooded with heat. 'Mind you, I don't blame you,' she continued. 'He's a sight for sore eyes, if only he was available.'

'He's not available?' Dani's heart sank like a stone. 'I hadn't heard that he was going out with anyone. Has the hospital grapevine actually missed out on some gossip?'

'Oh, it's not that he's going out with anyone so much as the fact that he rarely seems to go out with anyone more than a couple of times,' Nadia explained. 'That man is seriously dedicated to his job.'

'As if you aren't,' Dani countered, deliberately changing the direction of the conversation. 'You could almost be agoraphobic, because you never seem to leave the unit, let alone go outside the hospital.'

'So, I'm committed to my profession,' she said with an attempt at a dismissive shrug, obviously uncomfortable now that the focus was on her. 'I haven't noticed you racing for the door at the end of your shift either, but perhaps that's because you don't want to leave the gorgeous Mr Weatherby behind?'

If only she knew! Dani thought.

She'd never been one to clock-watch and had actually found herself lingering on the unit when she'd first joined Josh's team, just in the hope of seeing him or speaking to him. Now that she was sharing his flat, she'd become so aware of his presence that she was becoming afraid that she might inadvertently let him know exactly how she felt about him, and that wouldn't do. If she were to tell him that she loved him and wanted to spend the rest of her life with him, he would probably react in exactly the same way he had when she'd been eighteen, and that would destroy any headway she'd made in proving to him that she was now a grown woman who knew what she wanted.

No, she was going to have to take things slowly. This was a six-month placement and if she was patient, the idea of having her in his life permanently would grow on Josh until he couldn't bear for her to leave.

CHAPTER NINE

'CAITLIN, have you any idea where he's hiding?' Dani demanded, having wasted nearly half an hour trying to track Josh down before she resorted to speaking to his secretary.

'Your guess is as good as mine, on a Friday,' she said wryly. 'You know how manic it gets, with two separate clinics either side of lunch. All it needs is a couple of calls for consults down in A and E and everything goes to pot.'

'And there have been more than two today,' Dani admitted. She'd taken two herself, and had been grateful that neither of them had resulted in an admission to their unit. Unfortunately, she'd heard that Josh hadn't been so lucky, and the patient who had needed to be admitted for inpatient care had provoked another hasty round of musical beds while they'd tried to create a free cot.

'Have you tried paging him?' Caitlin asked distractedly, her hand already reaching for the phone that hardly ever seemed to stop ringing. 'He's usually pretty good about responding to that.'

Dani waved her thanks for the suggestion as she left the woman to her own particular chaos, but she really didn't want to page Josh. That would mean that she would probably end up speaking to him on the phone, and in spite of the fact that her query didn't honestly require a face-to-face conversation, it had been nearly three days since she'd last seen the man, and she was suffering serious withdrawal symptoms.

At least she could console herself with the fact that Josh obviously trusted her to be able to work without constant supervision, but that wasn't enough for her. It was a serious boost to her ego, this soon in her six-month placement, but quite apart from the fact that she was missing him, if she was ever going to rival him for excellence in this field, she wanted far more time working beside him so that she could benefit from his excellent teaching methods.

It wasn't until she was collecting her belongings and bundling herself up against the sudden storm that was dumping inches of rain over the area that she remembered that she had a means of contacting him that wouldn't raise any eyebrows around the hospital.

DaniD: Has BB turned into the Invisible Man?

She typed into the computer in his office once Caitlin had left for the day, having thought for several minutes before she could come up with a suitably light-hearted message.

She'd sent the message before another thought came to her, and she felt a grin spread over her face.

'Why didn't I think of that before?' she muttered as she set her fingers to the keys again.

DaniD: Am making world famous lasagne tonight. See you at eight?

He'd never be able to resist, she thought smugly, especially as he knew that she made his all-time favourite dish to his mother's recipe.

'Oh, help!' She'd just caught sight of the time. If she was going to be able to fulfil her boast, she was going to have to get her skates on. There was shopping to do before she could even start cooking, and as for dessert, she could make a decision about that while she was going round the shop. There definitely wasn't enough time to make panna cotta, or crème brûlée, but she might just be able to get her own version of lemon posset to set if she put individual bowls in the freezer while the lasagne was cooking.

It was lucky that she'd set the timer on the oven so that it would switch itself off at the end of the cooking time, otherwise, by the time she heard Josh's key in the door just before ten that night, the lasagne would have been burnt beyond salvaging.

Dani had spent the first hour waiting impatiently, wondering if she'd overdone her own preparations when she'd donned the silky lounging pyjamas that Meredith had given her for Christmas. She'd nearly gone and changed into her usual off-duty scruffs, except she hadn't wanted to be in her bedroom, half in and half out of her clothes when Josh walked through the door.

After that, it had been sheer stubbornness that had her sitting there waiting for him to come home before she had her own meal, determined that she would make him feel guilty that he hadn't at least phoned to let her know he was going to be late.

'Something smells good,' he said as he automatically turned to set the security lock on the door. 'Have you been cooking or did you resort to takeaway?'

Dani sat there with her mouth open, the angry words that had been boiling up in her for the last two hours completely forgotten when she caught sight of his drawn, ashen face. He looked so grim that she couldn't even feel disappointed that he hadn't so much as blinked at her slinky outfit.

'What's happened?' she demanded, leaping to her feet, her concern for him totally outweighing her pique that he hadn't bothered to contact her. 'Is it Meredith? Has something happened to Mum?'

'What? No!' he exclaimed. 'As far as I know, the two of them are still blissfully honeymooning.'

'So, what happened to make you look so…so grey?'

'Old age?' he quipped wearily. 'Or it could just be tiredness after a day of pointless meetings?'

'Or?' she prompted. 'I've seen you when you were so tired that you could barely put one foot in front of the other.'

'Or it could be the fact that we lost Marcus.'

'What?' Dani gasped in disbelief. The little boy hadn't been on the unit for very long, but had quickly stolen her heart. 'But he was responding to the antibiotics.'

'Apparently responding,' he countered dully as he slumped into the corner of the settee, the weight of the world on his shoulders. 'It must just have been his body's last desperate rally because his kidneys packed up completely, his temperature shot up through the roof and the infection in his lungs…' He didn't bother continuing, just shaking his head before he dropped it back against the upholstery and closed his eyes.

Dani didn't need him to say the words. She could all too easily picture the way poor little Marcus would have been struggling for every breath as the infection in his lungs had swiftly overwhelmed him, filling the spaces that should have held air with sticky, pervasive mucous so that in the end no life-giving oxygen would have been able to reach his struggling heart.

'What a waste!' Dani whispered, her throat clogged with tears. 'He was a beautiful, healthy little boy and he was absolutely perfect.'

'Sometimes life just doesn't seem to make much sense, does it?' Josh said, his voice rough with his own suppressed emotion. 'The whole situation was almost a carbon copy of what happened with Rosie, but in spite of the chaotic home birth, she recovered in a matter of days. Marcus was born in hospital and should have been safe, surrounded by all the latest high-tech equipment. Except there was a sudden influx of mums in labour and there just weren't enough midwives on duty.'

'Those poor parents,' Dani murmured, then remembered the inevitable consequence of such a death. 'Not only have they lost their son but they'll have to go through an inquest, too.'

'And the fact that we did everything possible to save him won't make any difference to the hospital's statistics—it will still put the unit's mortality rate up.'

'As if you care anything about statistics,' she scoffed. 'The only thing that matters to you is that Marcus died when his parents should be taking him home to the start of a long happy life.'

He opened his eyes just far enough for her to see the golden gleam, like catching a glimpse of candlelight through vintage brandy.

He looked at her for such a long time that Dani started to fidget, almost as if she was still the little girl who had found and eaten the last of his Easter egg but didn't know she had the chocolate smears around her face to give her away.

'What?' she asked when the silence stretched

a little too long for comfort, knowing that this time he couldn't be looking for chocolate while he gazed at her face.

'You've always known,' he said finally, the words so quiet that she wondered if he was even aware that he'd said them aloud.

'Known what?' she prompted softly, something deep inside her responding to the strange feeling of awareness that stretched between them.

'Known what makes me tick,' he said cryptically, then, in response to her frown, continued, 'You knew without me having to say anything that, in spite of the importance of those statistics to my unit, it would be the loss of the baby that would matter more.'

'It's how you've always been,' she said simply. 'That's why you spent so much time visiting me, when you could have resented me…rejected me, even…for taking Pammy away from you.'

'The thing I *did* resent was the fact that you were a girl,' he said gruffly. 'I'd convinced myself that Pammy was going to give me the little brother

I wanted. Danny was going to be someone I could teach to play football and ride a bike.'

'While the Dani you got instead pestered you until you learned how to do plaits in her hair and how to put bandages on her dolls,' she said with a chuckle. 'And I'm sorry if you were disappointed with what you got, but I wasn't in the least.'

'The best big brother in the world?' he suggested with a smug grin, but there was an unexpected edge to his voice when he said the familiar words, an edge accompanied by a strangely watchful expression that made her pulse take a sudden leap.

'Of course,' she agreed, because it was true, 'but not just that, because you were also a friend, a guide, a mentor, a bully, a tease—'

'Hey! I was quite enjoying the testimonial up to that point,' he complained, but she'd had to lighten the topic before she found herself voicing the thought that had just struck her—the fact that almost the only role he hadn't played in her life was that of lover.

She felt a wave of heat spread through her just at the thought of Josh as her lover.

While her classmates and friends had been going through the roller-coaster rides of first infatuations, first serious relationships and first sexual relationships, she'd been caught up in something entirely different…guilt-inducing daydreams about the man who had been her big brother for the whole of her life; impossible dreams, but they meant that there had never been anyone else who could measure up.

Of course, she'd tried to make herself forget him, to convince herself that it had all been nothing more than a childish infatuation that had got a little out of hand. Once or twice she'd even gone out with someone who wasn't him but it just hadn't worked.

Josh had always been the only one she'd ever wanted, and she'd fantasised about their first kiss for so long that she'd been hyperventilating before her lips had ever met his on that fateful birthday.

'Earth to Dani…!' Josh's voice was directed towards her through the makeshift megaphone of his hands. 'I said, have you already eaten, and if that gorgeous smell is lasagne, you'd better have left some for me, or retribution will be swift and ugly.'

'Oh! Lord! The lasagne!' Dani exclaimed and leapt to her feet, quickly seizing on an excuse to get away from the intensity of those sharp eyes even though she knew that the timer on the oven had switched it off long ago.

What on earth was the matter with her that she could have let herself sit there in front of the man fantasising about him? The last thing she wanted was for him to guess that her feelings were totally unchanged, not before she'd had a lot longer to get him accustomed to having her around.

'I knew it was lasagne!' he exclaimed behind her, and she nearly dropped the dish. 'Is it badly burnt? Can you just take the top layer off, or... Hey, it isn't burnt at all! When did you put it in the oven?'

'It was cooked and ready for eight,' she said as she slid it back into the oven and turning the heat back on to heat the dish through. 'I actually sent you a message to let you know, but things were obviously too hectic in the unit for you to see it in time.'

'And knowing just how likely a doctor is to be held up beyond the end of his shift, you took the precaution of setting the timer, thank goodness. It would have been a crime to let that get spoiled,' he said fervently. 'Now, what do you want me to do to help? Make a salad? Set the table?'

'How about having your shower while I get the rest of the meal ready?' she suggested, wondering if keeping herself busy would help to distract her from thinking about the fact that he was going to be standing naked under the pelting water just feet away from her. If she made enough noise, she might even be able to drown out the sound of the water running. Maybe then she wouldn't dream about him tonight.

'Are you sure? It doesn't seem fair that you should do all the preparations while I turn up late and take a shower.'

'You really don't think I've forgotten about the division of labour rule, do you?' She wagged a finger at him. 'The one who does the cooking doesn't have to do clean-up duty, so off you go and have your shower. I'll enjoy mine all the more after the meal, knowing you're stuck with the washing-up.'

The lasagne was one of the best she'd ever made and she hadn't been able to stop the stupid grin of satisfaction that spread over her face when Josh insisted on scraping the dish for any stray scraps.

It had been a lovely meal, and Dani was conscious that she was far more relaxed in his company than she'd been for a long time. Their conversation had ranged far and wide, inevitably circling back several times to events on the unit, but covering so many other topics that she'd probably never be able to recall half of them.

In fact, the whole evening would have been perfect if only she'd been able to stop her eyes constantly returning to his face, as fascinated as ever as she watched the expressions changing in his eyes as he spoke and fascinated, too, by his speed of thought and his command of language as he explained complicated medical concepts, inviting her to challenge his viewpoints even as he challenged hers.

She could have sat there hours longer, except she had work to do before she went to bed that night.

'I'd better get myself moving or it'll be the wee hours of the morning before I get to sleep,' she said finally.

'Why so late?' he said with a puzzled frown. 'It doesn't take you that long to have a shower, surely.'

'Hardly. It's the hours of study I've still got to do if I'm going to stand a chance of passing that next lot of exams first time.'

'Are you having trouble fitting the study in?' Suddenly he was the concerned consultant as well as the anxious big brother. 'The unit has been rather manically busy since you joined us.'

'I'll get there,' she reassured him as she stood and began to gather up the dirty plates and cutlery. 'If you can remember that far back, rather a lot of medical training is done on far too little sleep. I've done it before and I can do it again.'

'Cheeky madam!' he complained, before he

swiped the things out of her hands. 'Leave that to me and go have your shower.'

'Enjoy the clean-up,' she said with a teasing grin as she made her way out of the room. 'See you in the morning.'

Josh was nowhere to be seen when she made a quick foray into the kitchen for a glass of fruit juice and something to nibble on while she got her head down over her books.

'So much for putting your skimpiest nightie on…"just in case" you happened to bump into him,' she muttered under her breath as she grabbed a handful of grapes. Not that she was wearing anything particularly sexy. It wasn't really anything more than a glorified T-shirt, but the fine cotton knit clung to every curve and barely covered the essentials, even on someone of her height.

She padded back into her bedroom, cross with herself that she should have thought about doing something so juvenile.

'That's really the way to make him realise that

you're all grown up now,' she grumbled as she made her way towards the desk in the corner, then changed her mind and opted for the comfort of the bed.

It took a couple of journeys backwards and forwards to decide which books she was going to concentrate on this evening, and to switch on some Mozart, just in case it *did* increase brain power, then she realised that she'd left the grapes and the glass of juice on the desk and had to get up again to retrieve them.

Finally, she had everything just where she wanted it and slumped crossly against the headboard, only to catch the corner of the bedside cabinet with her elbow and send the glass of juice flying.

'Ah! No!' she gasped when she saw the liquid heading towards her most expensive recent purchase, a weighty tome detailing the principles and practice of caring for the premature baby.

At the very last second she managed to get her hand in position to deflect the glass and managed to spill the whole lot right down the front of herself.

Her gasp this time was one of shock as the cold liquid instantly soaked right through to her skin.

'Am I going to get *any* study done tonight?' she grumbled through gritted teeth as she scrambled off the bed before the liquid could soak into the bedclothes. One soaked mattress was more than enough.

At least she didn't have far to go to get to the bathroom, and another shower wouldn't take very long if she kept her hair out of the spray.

Without giving the matter another thought, she swung the bathroom door open and came to a shocked halt.

The last thing she'd expected to see was Josh standing stark naked in the shower with the water pelting down on him.

She must have made a sound because before she could back out of the room to leave him his privacy, his eyes sprang open and his hand flashed down to cover the fact that he was fully aroused.

Through the clear glass screen she saw his eyes widen as they travelled over her standing frozen in the doorway, and a glance into the mirror opposite her told her why. To her dismay she was suddenly aware of the fact that the fruit juice had not only plastered the fabric against her body but had turned it all but transparent.

Automatically her hands came up to hide her body, one at the juncture of her thighs and the other across her breasts, and if she hadn't been watching Josh's face she would never have seen the brief change in his expression or the shake of his head, neither would she have noticed the way his eyes darkened with an almost predatory hunger as his gaze travelled over her from head to toe.

Not that she wasn't doing some looking of her own, she realised as her eyes measured the unexpected muscularity of his naked body.

She'd seen him in his theatre scrubs often enough to know that his shoulders were broad and his arms were muscular, but she hadn't realised just how gorgeous he was without the covering of clothes, every curve and swell tight and solid and perfectly symmetrical, all the way down to his impressive six-pack and…

'Dani! *Don't!*' he growled, dragging her lascivious gaze up to his face and the pained expression on it.

Or *was* it pain?

Were his feelings anything like hers as he looked at her all-but-naked body? And he'd already been aroused *before* he'd seen her. Had her slinky pyjamas had more of an effect than she'd thought?

'Don't what?' she asked, and he must have been lip-reading because she didn't have enough breath to ask the question aloud.

'Don't look at me like that,' he ordered roughly, and closed his eyes to drop his head back against the wall of the shower with a shudder.

For the first time she noticed that there was no steam filling the walk-in enclosure and that, rather than a healthy pink glow to his skin from the warmth of the water, he was actually covered in goose-bumps.

'Josh?' For several embarrassing seconds she thought he was going to ignore her.

'What?' He was back to growling again and the

expression in his slitted eyes reminded her of one of the big-cat predators she'd seen on a wildlife programme. The stark similarity sent an atavistic shiver up her spine.

'Do cold showers actually work?'

He gave a startled huff of laughter then cast a grim glance down towards the hand still sheltering that most masculine portion.

'What do *you* think?' he said wryly.

'I think…I think I won't bother trying it as a remedy, then,' she said, hearing a new husky note to her own voice as she took a tentative step towards him. She snatched a quick breath for courage, forcing herself to hold his gaze as she took another step and then another as she continued speaking.

'I think you need to change the shower settings, to warm that water up a bit…and I think I need to take a warm shower, too, having spilled a glass of cold juice all over myself and…and I think it would definitely save water if we were to share the shower and…'

Her throat was so dry with nerves that she

couldn't continue, but by that time she was standing right in front of the curved glass panel of the shower.

'Dani,' Josh said, his tone clearly one of warning, but it was totally at odds with the expression in his eyes and on his face.

Summoning up the last of her courage, Dani reached for the hem of her wet T-shirt and stripped it swiftly over her head, then felt a sudden surge of unexpected power when she saw the way every muscle and sinew in his body grow tense in response.

'Are you going to let me in?' she asked, her voice little more than a whisper as she put one foot onto the icy shower floor.

'Dammit, Dani…' Josh began, but this time she wasn't going to take no for an answer, not when it was obviously what they both wanted.

'Warm the water up, quickly,' she interrupted with a shaky attempt at a smile. 'Blue is only a good colour if you're wearing it, not if you're turning blue with the cold.'

His answering smile was faint, but her heart

leapt when he reached out obediently with his free hand to turn the control.

As far as she was concerned, that was tacit permission to join him, and she stepped fully into the enclosure and straight into his welcoming arms.

'Oh!' she gasped when he tugged her against his slick wet body. 'You're so cold!'

'You're not much warmer,' he growled. 'How did you get so wet?' Both arms tightened around her and she realised that one part of his anatomy certainly wasn't cold, no matter how long he'd been standing under the freezing shower.

'I had to save my book from the juice...but at least, this time, the mattress didn't get soaked.'

Her mind wasn't really on what she was saying. What did conversation matter when she was finally where she'd wanted to be for so many years?

And it felt so good.

The closest she'd come to seeing him naked had been the time she'd walked in on him changing his shirt and the glimpses she caught of his chest when he leaned forward at the operating table...unless you counted the trips to the swimming pool when he had been teaching her five-year-old self to swim.

From her early teens, ever since she'd first fallen in love with him, she'd imagined what it would feel like when he finally held her in his arms, but this surpassed anything she'd ever dreamed. He was so tall and strong—the sort of solid bulwark that a woman could depend on to protect her when life turned rough. And his skin felt like slick satin under her fingers as she traced the rivulets of warm water over his shoulders and down across the flat swells of his pectorals.

It was only when her exploring fingertip reached the dark disc of his nipple, almost hidden in the thicket of dark tawny hair, that she realised that any pretence at conversation had ceased. In fact, there was complete silence in the cubicle apart from the hiss and splash of water…not even the sound of her jagged breathing registered over the sound of her suddenly racing heart.

Instantly, she was convinced that the tension she could feel in Josh's body was the signal that history was about to repeat itself, and even though everything inside her screamed at her to prolong this moment of delight for as long as possible, honesty told her that she had to look up at him.

She didn't want to, because she would know what he was going to say as soon as she saw his expression, so she took her time about reaching her destination, enjoying her last chance to be this close to the dark swathe of hair across the width of his chest and the erotic way that hair felt as it brushed against her nipples. The hollow at the base of his throat seemed strangely vulnerable, especially with the beat of his pulse so visible there, and the angle of his jaw seemed sharper than ever, a clear indication that that he was gritting his teeth…steeling himself to find the right words to push her away and restore the proper distance between them?

Then she met his eyes and when the heat in them almost incinerated her on the spot, she realised that she'd had absolutely no idea what he was really thinking.

'Dani…' Her name rumbled up from the depths

inside him and she was fascinated to realise that with her body plastered against his, she could actually feel the vibration of it in her own chest.

'I'm sorry,' he muttered, almost incoherently, as his head swooped down towards her, even as he swept her up into his arms and pressed his lips to hers.

At last!

The words sang inside her as she wrapped her arms around his neck and gave herself up to the overwhelming sensation.

This was nothing like her clumsy attempt on her eighteenth birthday. This was the first kiss they'd ever shared and it was everything that she'd imagined and more. Her pulse was racing and she suddenly seemed to be filled with hot glittery sparkles until she almost felt as if she was going to burst into flames.

They were both panting now, uncaring that the water was pouring down on them as they tilted their heads this way and that, desperate to take the kiss deeper and deeper.

And still she wanted more—*needed* more—

needed to become an intrinsic part of this magnificent man until neither of them could tell where one ended and the other began.

Dani was trembling so hard that she had to wrap her legs around him, too, her system going into overload as she went beyond anything that her imagination had been able to conjure up.

He seemed to be everywhere around her, one arm supporting her shoulders as he plundered her mouth as though starving for the taste of her, the other arm supporting her weight as though it was nothing, pressing her against the solid warmth of his obviously male, obviously heavily aroused body.

She had never realised just how overwhelming the elemental desire between a man and a woman could be, and for just a moment, as she felt him poised for the first time at the entrance to her body, fear of the unknown took over as she realised that they had reached a life-changing moment.

'Dani?'

She gave a mew of displeasure when he tore his mouth away from hers and leaned back just far enough to force her to look up at him, apparently unaware…or uncaring… that the movement also pressed their lower bodies much closer together.

'We shouldn't be doing this,' he rasped, the sound so raw that the words might have been torn out of him. 'Tell me now and I'll stop,' he declared, even as his hand tightened convulsively on her bottom, giving the lie to the promise.

CHAPTER TEN

STOP? She shook her head while she gazed fiercely into his golden predator's eyes. That was the last thing she wanted to do. Not when it had taken her nearly a decade to get here.

But she knew that he *would* do it if she asked it of him, even though he had reached this stage of intimacy, and if he should even guess that she'd been waiting for him…that he was the first…the *only* man with whom she'd shared such intimacies…

That realisation told her that she would have to do something very deliberate to convince him that this was absolutely what she wanted.

Without releasing his gaze, she took one hand from around his neck and reached down to position his impressive masculinity where instinct told her it should be, then tightened her legs around his lean hips and deliberately began to impale herself on him.

She saw the pupils of his eyes widen and darken even as she trembled in anticipation of the pain that teenage whispers had told her to expect. Was she going to be brave enough to inflict that on herself, to drive herself onto him to destroy the final proof of her innocence?

And then the decision was taken away from her as he palmed each of her hips in his strong supple hands to brace her for his desperate thrust.

Her sharp whimper of dismay was followed instantly by his shocked expletive.

'You're a virgin!' he accused, disbelief almost insultingly clear on his face and every muscle and sinew as rigid as iron.

'Not any more,' she pointed out with an attempt at levity, suddenly horribly aware that she might have totally miscalculated. If Josh rejected her now, she didn't think she would ever be able to recover.

'Dammit, Dani…'

'And if you're even thinking of stopping at this point, I will definitely have to kill you,' she continued, refusing to allow him to speak. Then she concentrated on experimentally tightening the muscles deep inside her, the ones that were being stretched for the very first time to accommodate their intended purpose. She was delighted to discover that while there was a slight throb of discomfort, there certainly wasn't any hint of debilitating pain.

In fact, as she deliberately squeezed the muscles again, she wondered if that throb might actually be something to do with the amazing sensation of fullness that having Josh buried inside her would have to produce.

'You're impossible,' he said on a groan when she tightened around him for a third time, his long fingers flexing and tightening around her hips as though tempted almost beyond bearing.

'Actually,' Dani said in a throaty voice she'd never heard coming out of her mouth before, 'that was my thought, exactly, when I caught my first glimpse of you…that it would be impossible for something that big to fit…'

'Dani!' He gave a huff of laughter and she was amazed to see that she'd actually embarrassed him.

'Good for the ego?' she teased, but didn't give him any time to come up with an answer as she deliberately loosened her hold on his shoulders and hips so that her body started to slide further down him, and on him.

In a swift move that stole her breath, he whirled around to press her back against the wall of the shower, his body curving over her to shelter her from the shower spray as he gazed fiercely at her.

'You're good for my ego and everything else that ails me,' he declared, and she gave a shiver of awareness when she realised just how vulnerable her position was if she hadn't trusted him completely. 'Unfortunately, this time you've goaded me too far and I'm already on a hair trigger.' He flexed his hips and she was suddenly torn between the need to retreat from his invasion—an absolute impossibility with the wall behind her—and the overwhelming desire to arch her body towards his to take everything he had to give.

'So, promise that next time will be just for me,' she suggested in a wicked whisper, and gave herself over to the maelstrom.

Was that the alarm? Josh thought groggily as something electronic tried to summon him from the depths of sleep.

He cracked an eye open to look at the time then let his head drop heavily back onto the pillow when he calculated that it had been little more than an hour since he and Dani had finally succumbed to exhaustion.

He felt a satisfied smile creep over his face when he tried to remember exactly how many times they'd—

The thought was cut off abruptly when his phone began to ring and he realised that it had been his mobile that had dragged him to wakefulness. It was awkward reaching for it with Dani curled against his side but he certainly didn't want to disturb her. It just felt too good to have her there with her head on his shoulder and her hand over his heart.

'H'lo,' he growled, resenting the fact that such a call at this time of the morning meant he was unlikely to have time to do anything about his burgeoning arousal. Surely he should be too exhausted to grow so hard so quickly, but it seemed as if all he had to do was look at that surprisingly womanly little body to want her all over again.

'Josh, I'm sorry to call you, but we're going to need you,' said the voice on the other end, and he instantly switched his focus. His patients deserved nothing less than his total concentration.

'What have you got?' He spared a single regretful glance as he slid gently out from her slender weight and padded towards the bathroom that had been the epicentre of the explosion last night.

A quick detour to collect a fresh set of clothes only took seconds but it was long enough for a recitation of the basic facts.

'What have you tried to control the contractions? And how high is her blood pressure? Is it coming down at all?' he demanded as he began to form a clearer picture of the risks two tiny babies were facing.

'OK, I'll be with you in fifteen minutes... twenty at the outside. Has Theatre been warned that she might need to get in there in a hurry? Cross your fingers that we don't. If there's any chance of delaying things, we need every second we can manage to get some steroids into her. And warn the unit that we'll need a warmed humidicrib, just in case.'

'Twenty-six weeks, dammit!' he swore, almost throwing the phone down as he strode towards the shower. That was far too soon for babies to arrive in the world. Their little bodies just weren't ready to take on the rigours of doing their own breathing.

For a second, as he reached out to the controls, he contemplated turning them to cold to try to dispel the lingering mists of sleep.

'Don't you dare!' Dani grumbled sleepily as she followed him into the walk-in enclosure and flipped the lever on full before coming under the deluge of warm water with him. 'Tell me about the patient,' she demanded, somehow managing to speak and rinse her hair without getting a mouthful of soap.

Josh hadn't even realised that she was following him, and was delighted that she seemed to have automatically presumed that he would want her to come to the hospital with him. He found himself reciting the information he'd gleaned so far, stunned to discover that he could actually share the shower with this beautiful naked water-sprite without his brain totally shutting down to everything but the need to make love with her all over again.

Was that because her attitude towards him this morning was so totally matter-of-fact, making their sharing of the shower seem like nothing more erotic than a convenient means of saving time?

'Twins. Twenty-six weeks gestation,' he told her briefly, focusing once more on the situation waiting for them. 'Mother's started having contractions and her blood pressure's gone up, but we're still waiting for tests to tell us whether that's stress-related or eclampsia or a kidney infection or…whatever other complication pregnancy can throw up at us.'

'But you're thinking we might end up with two more patients in the very near future?' She stepped out of the shower and reached for a towel, giving him a swift view of her perfect heart-shaped bottom before it disappeared behind the nubby cloth.

'That's usually what happens when I get calls at this time of night,' he said heavily as he flipped the water off and exited the enclosure to grab his own towel. 'It's rarely good news.'

'Unfortunately,' she added, distractedly scrubbing at her hair with the towel as she hurried through the door that led into her own room, obviously in a quest for clean clothes.

Josh reached for his deodorant and knocked several other items off the shelf, only realising what they were when the little foil-wrapped packages spilled across the vanity unit.

For several stunned seconds he stared down at

them in horrified fascination, only then taking in the fact that he'd never once thought about using them last night.

His mind was so full of his discovery that he reached for his ringing phone without conscious thought, unable to decide whether his initial reaction had been dread or delight.

'Yes?' he said, unforgivably distracted by the image of Dani's slender body swollen with his child.

'Full-blown eclampsia,' said the voice on the other end of the phone. 'She's on her way to Theatre for an emergency Caesarean.'

Josh swore fluently, not certain whether the worst of his invective was for the babies that might die before he could even reach the hospital or for the baby that might even now be in its earliest stages deep inside Dani.

Dammit, how could he have been so careless? As if it wasn't bad enough to have taken her virginity, he might even have impregnated her at the same time.

'What's the hold-up?' the object of his guilty

thoughts demanded from the doorway. 'Was that the hospital? What's the latest situation?'

'Eclampsia,' he said gruffly, having to drag his eyes away from the slenderness of her waist as he realised with a sudden surge of possessiveness that he fiercely wanted her to be pregnant; that the cave-man in him could think of nothing more wonderful than to know that the seed he'd planted inside her during the night would grow into the perfect combination of the two of them.

He drove them to the hospital, the early hour meaning that traffic would be light enough for them to make good time, but to Dani's surprise, the journey took place in complete silence.

Well, he was probably thinking about the babies that were even now being brought into the world to save the life of their mother, she rationalised, even as she was remembering the shocked expression she'd glimpsed on his face as he'd gazed down at the condoms littered across the vanity unit.

She'd been shocked, too.

She'd never even given pregnancy a thought until that moment, or the possibility of contracting a sexually transmitted disease…and she was supposed to be a responsible medical professional, for heaven's sake!

Inside her head she heard a hollow laugh.

As if doctors were any less likely than anybody else to get carried away by hormone overload. In fact, the more she thought about it, the fact that medicine was such a high-stress occupation probably made it all the more likely that they would grab at the chance to indulge in the release of such a basically life-affirming activity.

She blew a mental raspberry at her self-serving rationalisation, knowing that it had been nothing more than greed that had made her so forgetful. She'd seen her chance to make love with Josh and she'd grabbed at it, regardless of any consequences.

And if she had become pregnant some time between the first time against the shower wall, the second time on the vanity counter—when they hadn't even been able to get out of the bathroom before desire had overtaken them again—and all the other times they'd reached for the stars once they'd finally made it to his bed?

Well, if Josh's baby was already taking shape deep inside her, a microscopic bundle of rapidly dividing cells, she would have some decisions to make. Not about whether she would keep the baby, because there was absolutely no question about that. No, there would be other choices to be made, about the change in direction her career would have to take if she were to become a single parent.

Her heart ached at that thought, knowing it was the last thing she would want for her child. Meredith had been the best mother she could have wished for, but she'd always been so certain that one day she would have a *real* family, with two parents to share the joys and pains of parenthood.

She flicked a quick glance in Josh's direction as he manoeuvred into a slot in the staff car park and wondered just how long it would be before he had time to speak to her…to bring up the matter of the forgotten birth control, because she knew without a shadow of a doubt that he *would* bring it up. She also knew that his over-developed sense of responsibility towards her, honed from the first second he'd seen her in that special care baby unit all those years ago, would probably lead him to make all sorts of promises that he didn't need to make.

No, she was absolutely determined that one thing was *not* up for discussion, no matter what else happened. She may have been in love with Josh for more than half her life, and she would have loved nothing more than to spend the rest of her life with him, if this had been anything more than a sexual encounter fuelled by proximity and more than a hint of stupidity, but there was no way that she would ever use a pregnancy to trap him into marriage.

We didn't use a condom. Not once.

Josh knew he should feel utterly guilty for the oversight and for the fact that it could be responsible for derailing the career Dani had fought so long and hard for. But it was very difficult to feel more than a twinge of remorse when everything inside him was soaring at the thought that his lack of forethought might have resulted in a pregnancy.

Of course, he could try to excuse himself with the probability that a woman of her age was more than likely to be on the Pill, and reason with himself that *that* was why she hadn't felt the need to mention protection, but there was no point dwelling on it now. In fact, he shouldn't be thinking about it at all.

He should be thinking about those two little babies and going over lists in his head to be certain that he wouldn't miss anything in their care, but to be perfectly honest, this was something he'd done so often that the basic organisation was all but automatic. Then, too, there was the fact that he had a staff that was probably second to none in the specialist care of these fragile little beings, every one of them hand-picked and utterly dedicated.

No, he'd far rather dwell on the possibility that those hours of mind-blowing pleasure, when he'd filled Dani with his seed over and over again, had started the miracle of a whole new life.

Even now, he could hardly believe that it had happened. In so many dreams through countless harrowing days and during nights shattered by the loss of patients for whom he had never been able to do enough, it had always been Dani shining in the darkness like a lodestar.

He should have been mortified to have her walk into the bathroom and find him so obviously aroused, but the expression in her eyes had been exactly like the one in his imagination and he'd given up the will to resist.

A final warning had gone off in his head as he'd pulled her into his arms, but it had been too little and much too late. He'd claimed her mouth, kissing her over and over, the mere fact of having her in his arms at last making him ache with a need more intense than he'd ever known, and when she'd…

'Thank God you're here,' the anaesthetist said fervently as soon as the lift doors slid open, and that train of thought was derailed for the foreseeable future.

'The two babies are alive, so far,' the haggard

man reported, his scrubs looking as if he'd slept in them, even though the shadows under his eyes proved that he hadn't.

'Obs and Gyn on-call did a good job getting them out so quickly when she arrested,' he continued, 'but the mother's not looking much better yet. She's in ICU and I've got to get back to her, but you've got some serious juggling to do if you're going to make room in your unit. Either that, or you'll have to find another unit to take them,' he added as he strode away, his clogs clunking noisily all the way down the corridor.

Transfer such vulnerable babies to another unit? Not if he could help it, he vowed silently as he automatically began the rigorous hand-cleaning routine outside the glass-walled heart of the unit. Without being arrogant about it, he knew that they would have a better than average chance of survival with the least possible number of side-effects to their premature arrival if they stayed here, so what he had to do now was work out how he could make that happen.

'Dani!' Nadia exclaimed. 'I knew Josh had been called in because the babies' father is a member of staff at the hospital, but I didn't know you'd been called in, too.' Josh saw the swift wash of hectic colour flood into Dani's face, her pale complexion making her embarrassment impossible to hide.

She threw a panicky glance at him, clearly at a loss to explain her presence without revealing their current living arrangements.

'Dani and I happen to live in the same block of flats,' he said perfectly truthfully, much as he would have liked to stake a public claim to her. 'I gave her a lift in, knowing it was going to be utter chaos while we play pass-the-parcel with the babies.'

He reached out to the box of disposable gloves. 'So, let's get down to it,' he said briskly while he began his own assessment of their newest charges, double-checking everything that had happened to them so far. 'I need a rundown on each of the babies so we can decide who's ready to graduate to the tender mercies of Paeds.'

* * *

It was more than an hour before things began to be organised to his satisfaction, and still several hours before either he or Dani was officially due on duty, when he finally made his way to his office.

They were still waiting for a specially equipped ambulance to arrive to take one little boy back to the hospital nearest to his family home, and Josh knew that he would probably have to make more than a few visits to the little girl who'd been transferred to the paediatric department at the other end of the children's wing, but it looked as if the current crisis had been brought under control.

Now it was time to deal with the potential crisis brewing in his private life, and he'd do that just as soon as Dani answered her page.

He swore aloud, cursing himself for getting into this situation in the first place.

'I should know better,' he said angrily, then realised just how crazy that sounded. Doctors were just as likely as any other member of society to get carried away, especially when they'd been waiting as long as he had to make love with Dani.

And he could honestly say that he hadn't given a single thought to protection once he'd seen her standing there with those big dark blue eyes travelling over his naked body with that hot hungry expression in them.

The memory of that expression made him burn anew, his body responding fast enough to make him feel light-headed as so much of his blood headed south.

'Damn, you'd think I'd be exhausted after the number of times we reached for each other during the night,' he muttered. In fact, they should both have been close to comatose and in need of oxygen therapy if their hunger for each other hadn't seemed to redouble with the slightest contact, and Dani's ego-boosting eagerness had let him know that she had been every bit as ravenous.

Even thinking about what they'd experienced together made him desperate for more, but he had something far more permanent in mind than an affair, even if that affair was hot enough to blister the paint off the walls.

Josh groaned as he leant back in his chair and contemplated the impossible task in front of him.

He knew that there were a multitude of reasons why the whole situation was wrong. He *was* too old for her, and they *had* been brought up as brother and sister, and the hospital *could* see it as evidence of sexual harassment if a consultant were to become involved with a junior member of staff in his department.

But...

He sighed heavily when he tried to envision a future without Dani at the centre of it...especially if she was already carrying his child.

Could he be happy if he were to keep himself on the very edge of her life, keeping an eye on her without asking for any more intimate involvement? That would leave her free to find a man of her own age and fall in love and...

'No!' Black jealousy clawed at his heart at the possibility of another man touching Dani, and he knew that he would never be able to stand aside and watch it happen.

'So, what's the alternative?' he asked the four

walls, glad that Caitlin hadn't arrived yet to hear him talking to himself.

'I suppose what I've got to do is find a way to persuade Dani that we *could* make a go of it.' He squeezed his eyes shut and tried to imagine the expression on her face if he asked her to marry him.

Would she be shocked?

She'd certainly been willing enough to make love with him last night, but would she be equally willing to commit herself to a lifetime together? She'd worked so hard, fought to be independent, and he might have spoiled everything with his selfish forgetfulness.

So, should he suggest that they just move in together, take things a step at a time until she was so accustomed to living together that she wouldn't balk when he suggested marriage?

A familiar tap at the door told him that Dani had arrived and for a second his heart was beating so fast that he could hardly draw enough breath to speak.

* * *

Dani heard Josh's voice call her in, but it took her several seconds before she could bring herself to open the door.

She'd already spent ten minutes in the staff cloakroom psyching herself up for this meeting.

Oh, she knew exactly what he was going to say…that he was sorry, and that it should never have happened, and that if she thought about it sensibly, she would realise that he was far too old for her, and that she needed to find someone her own age and fall in love and have the perfect family she'd always wanted, and so on, and so on.

But she didn't want anyone else. She'd never wanted anyone else, and even if they had been brought up as brother and sister, it certainly hadn't felt like it last night and there was absolutely no blood relationship between them.

In fact, apart from the fact that he still had that whole protective thing going, she hadn't thought of him as a brother since she'd reached her teens. And as for the age difference, it hadn't stopped them enjoying themselves, neither had it affected his stamina.

'Come in,' Josh repeated with more than a hint of impatience, and she snatched a quick breath as she crossed her fingers and opened the door.

He was sitting formally behind his desk with his hands linked on the blotter and she was so nervous about meeting his eyes and seeing the confirmation that he was going to return to their old relationship that she concentrated on those hands.

She loved his hands; had always been fascinated by them from the days when he would fix her dolls and brush and plait her hair for school. They were lean and deceptively elegant and, oh, so sensitive when it came to treating their little patients...or making love...

And any moment he was going to tell her that she could never have what she wanted; that it was totally impossible.

But it wasn't impossible. Nothing as special as what they'd shared last night could ever be impossible. They were meant to be together. They'd always been meant to be together, right from the first moment when he'd seen her as a tiny baby and decided to learn how to help her to live. They'd already wasted years when they could have been together, making each other happy.

'Dani?' His deep voice demanded that she finally meet his gaze, but it took more courage than she'd realised. His eyes seemed darker than usual and more intent and it felt as if a fist was clenched tight around her heart as she waited for him to start speaking the fateful words.

'Marry me,' he demanded simply, and she stared at him in utter disbelief.

'Wh-what?' she gulped, certain that she must have mistaken what he'd said, turning it into what she wanted to hear instead.

Oh, and they *were* the words she wanted to hear, more than anything.

'You *must*, Dani,' Josh said heatedly. 'After last night…'

Dani's heart had leapt at his apparent eagerness only to crash to earth when she realised what was really going on here.

After last night, when they hadn't taken any precautions, there was every likelihood that she could be pregnant. *That* was why he'd just proposed. It was that damned over-developed sense of responsibility, not the realisation that he'd fallen in love with her and couldn't live without her.

'No,' she said with a quiver of agony in her voice, hardly able to believe that she was turning down the one thing she'd wanted for more than half her life.

For a fraction of a second it almost looked as if her refusal had hurt him, but then he closed his eyes and she couldn't be sure.

'Dani…' There was determination visible in his expression now, but was she guilty of wishful thinking to imagine that she could still see a hint of vulnerability?

'You only asked because Mum will give you hell if she finds out what we did,' she accused, even as she hoped desperately that he would deny it. And, of course, he did.

'Actually, I hadn't even thought about that,' he said with a wry expression. 'But that wasn't why I proposed.'

'No?' Her legs were shaking and she was really beginning to wish that she'd made herself comfortable when she'd first entered the room. Now she was left feeling a bit like a pupil called onto the carpet in the headmaster's room. 'So, why did you? Just because there's a chance I might be pregnant?'

He surged to his feet, clearly short of patience after a night with very little sleep and a stressful wake-up call, and his fierce expression made her take an involuntary step back. 'Because I've reached the point where I'll take any chance I can get,' he declared.

Chance? Dani frowned, suddenly feeling as if she'd just lost track of the conversation. 'What chance?'

'The chance to tie you to me, of course.' He looked almost shamefaced at the admission as he dragged impatient fingers through his hair, leaving it sticking up in every direction.

'Look, Dani, I know I'm far too old for you and—apart from that spectacular lapse last night—you've probably never thought of me as anything other than your big brother, but that's not the way I've been thinking about you for so long that—'

'It was rather spectacular, wasn't it?' she interrupted, with her heart taking off like a hot-air balloon inside her, certain that her smile must stretch from ear to ear when she realised just what he'd just admitted. 'I was so worried that the fact it was my first time would put you off. I never dreamed that making love would be so…'

'Dani,' he groaned. 'Stop it.'

'Stop what?'

'Stop looking at me like that,' he growled.

'Like what?' she asked with a pretence at innocence, starting to enjoy this new game between them.

'You know very well what I mean,' he grumbled. 'You look as if you want to…'

'As if I want to eat you up?' she suggested wickedly, and he groaned.

'You can't say things like that. Not here,' he insisted with a wary glance towards Caitlin's door.

'Why not, if they're true?' she asked simply, and because she just couldn't wait to touch him again, when only moments ago she'd believed that she would have to leave the hospital and put him out of her life for good, she quickly made her way round to his side of the desk.

She was delighted when he immediately pulled her onto his lap to cradle her head against his shoulder, and touched when she realised that his whole body was trembling just as much as hers.

'Ah, Dani, I really hope you've thought this through, that you're sure…'

'Josh, this is something very special. It's not going to go away—ever—and neither am I.'

'You sound very certain,' he challenged, tilting her head back so that she was looking up into his face and could see that he was serious.

'I couldn't be more certain. Face it, Josh, we're meant to be together.' She traced his clever mouth with a fingertip, shivering as she remembered some of the things that mouth had done to her last night. 'We've always been meant for each other,' she said, aware that the tone of her voice had changed with her growing arousal. 'We've wasted years when we could have been together, making each other happy, and we're not going to waste any more. Where's the point when you love me and I love you and—?'

'They weren't wasted, Dani, not if they gave you time to qualify for a profession you love. But you do realise that we can't rush into anything, don't you? We'll have to wait until the honeymooners return,' he pointed out, clearly distracted by her exploring fingers. 'They'd never forgive us if we made any arrangements without them.'

'So give them a ring and tell them to hurry back,' Dani demanded, silently cursing the fact that this conversation was taking place in his office when all she could think about was taking his clothes off again and taking her explorations further. 'After all, if they don't get here soon, I'll be too pregnant to fit into a wedding dress.'

'You're that certain that I made you pregnant last night?' The scientist in him seemed quite fascinated by the idea.

'Last night, tonight, tomorrow night...' She shrugged nonchalantly. 'We're almost bound to get it right one night if we keep practising.'

'And you wouldn't mind that?' He captured her hand, silently demanding her whole attention for the question. 'After all your training? And when you're so close to achieving your goal?'

'Josh, medicine is my career, my profession, my *calling*, if you want to label it that. I have confidence that I'm good at it and, anyway, even if I *am* pregnant, there's time for me to take this next lot of exams. And I can always return to it sooner or later if I *do* take time off to have babies. But there is only one thing I really need to make me feel complete, and that's you.'

'Oh, Dani, what did I ever do to deserve you?' he whispered against her lips before he kissed her. And this was a kiss that was different from any that had gone before. It held an acceptance that this really was where they were meant to be.

MEDICAL™

Large Print

Titles for the next six months...

September

THE CHILDREN'S DOCTOR'S SPECIAL PROPOSAL	Kate Hardy
ENGLISH DOCTOR, ITALIAN BRIDE	Carol Marinelli
THE DOCTOR'S BABY BOMBSHELL	Jennifer Taylor
EMERGENCY: SINGLE DAD, MOTHER NEEDED	Laura Iding
THE DOCTOR CLAIMS HIS BRIDE	Fiona Lowe
ASSIGNMENT: BABY	Lynne Marshall

October

A FAMILY FOR HIS TINY TWINS	Josie Metcalfe
ONE NIGHT WITH HER BOSS	Alison Roberts
TOP-NOTCH DOC, OUTBACK BRIDE	Melanie Milburne
A BABY FOR THE VILLAGE DOCTOR	Abigail Gordon
THE MIDWIFE AND THE SINGLE DAD	Gill Sanderson
THE PLAYBOY FIREFIGHTER'S PROPOSAL	Emily Forbes

November

THE SURGEON SHE'S BEEN WAITING FOR	Joanna Neil
THE BABY DOCTOR'S BRIDE	Jessica Matthews
THE MIDWIFE'S NEW-FOUND FAMILY	Fiona McArthur
THE EMERGENCY DOCTOR CLAIMS HIS WIFE	Margaret McDonagh
THE SURGEON'S SPECIAL DELIVERY	Fiona Lowe
A MOTHER FOR HIS TWINS	Lucy Clark

MILLS & BOON

MEDICAL™

Large Print

December

THE GREEK BILLIONAIRE'S LOVE-CHILD	Sarah Morgan
GREEK DOCTOR, CINDERELLA BRIDE	Amy Andrews
THE REBEL SURGEON'S PROPOSAL	Margaret McDonagh
TEMPORARY DOCTOR, SURPRISE FATHER	Lynne Marshall
DR VELASCOS' UNEXPECTED BABY	Dianne Drake
FALLING FOR HER MEDITERRANEAN BOSS	Anne Fraser

January

THE VALTIERI MARRIAGE DEAL	Caroline Anderson
THE REBEL AND THE BABY DOCTOR	Joanna Neil
THE COUNTRY DOCTOR'S DAUGHTER	Gill Sanderson
SURGEON BOSS, BACHELOR DAD	Lucy Clark
THE GREEK DOCTOR'S PROPOSAL	Molly Evans
SINGLE FATHER: WIFE AND MOTHER WANTED	Sharon Archer

February

EMERGENCY: WIFE LOST AND FOUND	Carol Marinelli
A SPECIAL KIND OF FAMILY	Marion Lennox
HOT-SHOT SURGEON, CINDERELLA BRIDE	Alison Roberts
A SUMMER WEDDING AT WILLOWMERE	Abigail Gordon
MIRACLE: TWIN BABIES	Fiona Lowe
THE PLAYBOY DOCTOR CLAIMS HIS BRIDE	Janice Lynn

™ MILLS & BOON®